Mommy's Always Here

An MDLG and ABDL story about meeting the perfect person at the wrong time and how the love of a Mommy can help heal all wounds

By Tina Moore

Table of Contents

Chapter 1

There was no explaining how Leila felt. She was numb. The swirling world around her seemed so full of life, so happy, so content that it almost made her sick. Leila had just broken up with her Mommy after spending six years together. It was mutual, that's what Leila kept telling herself, but deep down she knew that it wasn't. Leila had put on weight over the last two years, and that was something Donna couldn't look past. Leila hated herself for it, but what she hated, even more, was that she didn't have the control or discipline to stop herself. It's not as though she ate particularly unhealthy foods, but with her new job and moving to a new city, her exercise routine had gone out of the window. What was more was that Leila was about to celebrate her 36th birthday.

Who, in their right mind, would want an overweight, 36-year-old as their baby? I will never find someone who will want me. I'm not what other women look for. I'm not what they want, Leila thought as she took the train to her new apartment. She had moved out of the home she and Donna had bought together and moved into a small, one-bedroom apartment just outside of town. Leila looked around the train and sighed.

How could she have been so cruel? I never even did anything to deserve that treatment, Leila asked herself, catching her reflection in the window of the train as it went through a tunnel. Looking away out of disgust, Leila tried to fight back her tears.

Idiot. You're a fucking idiot. She called herself as she stood up and made her way to the door, ready to get out. There was the usual hustle and bustle of the impatient people as she disembarked and felt the push come behind her, knocking her to the floor. People swarmed around her, but not to help, simply to get to where they needed to be. Leila looked up, sighing and resting her hands on her knees as she looked around.

I'm invisible, no one is ever going to notice

me, and I mean, why should they, I'm nothing, she sadly thought, picking up her bag and putting it back on her shoulder before standing up and walking out of the station.

Leila walked down the street, looking over her hands and taking off the ring Donna had given her as a present.

"I won't be needing this anymore," Leila said out loud. She was just about to put it in the bin when she saw a young homeless woman and decided that she would have better use for the ring than the bin.

"Here," Leila said to the girl wrapped in rags. The girl looked up at her in shock. Something about her sparkly eyes made Leila catch her breath, and as the girl gingerly accepted the ring, Leila smiled despite herself.

"I can't take this," the girl said, standing up and pushing the ring back into Leila's hands. Leila frowned and watched the woman scurry down the street.

"Wait, stop," Leila said, catching her breath

as she turned the corner to follow the woman just to be stopped by three police officers. Leila froze, her heart pounding, and her cheeks flushed red. She saw the homeless woman behind them, taking off her rags and letting her hair out. Leila wasn't sure if it was the run or the beauty of the woman, which kept her cheeks burning red, but as the woman walked back over to her, the answer was clear. The woman was tall, athletic, and in her late 20's from what Leila could tell. She had shoulder-length blonde hair and eyes that seemed so warm and loving.

"This is why I couldn't accept your ring," the woman said, her voice deep and smoldering.

"I see," Leila said, blushing with embarrassment.

"You're sweet. But, you might have messed up what we were doing if you had kept insisting," the woman explained, making Leila roll her eyes and nod.

"This is just the perfect end to the kind of day I've had. Sorry," Leila said before smiling once more and turning to walk away.

"Wait," the woman said, thinking for a moment before jogging after Leila.

"I'm Avery, but everyone calls me Avs," Avery said, extending her hand and waiting for Leila to shake it.

"I'm Leila," Leila replied, enjoying how Avery's hand seemed to make hers look small.

"What are you doing later? Like nowish?" Avery asked, taking Leila by surprise.

"I was thinking, drinks, and dinner, maybe?" Avery said, making Leila laugh in surprise.

"Um, yeah, sure," Leila said, shaking her head, surprised that the beautiful fit cop wanted to hang out with her.

"Sweet. Just give me like five minutes," Avery said, winking at Leila before running back to her colleagues.

"So, do you live around here? I guess you don't come from around here, you're voice to refined," Avery said, making Leila laugh.

"I've been called a lot of things, never once refined though," Leila replied as they walked. It was just on dusk, and the lights of the city started flickering on. This was Leila's favorite time of day when the transition between day and night made the city glow.

"I'm not from around here, no. I moved here recently. After a break-up," Leila said. She was nervous that Avery might want to stop it right there and then, she didn't seem to be the person who enjoyed being a rebound.

"No, I get it. I moved precincts when I broke up with my ex. That was like, seven months ago now. We were only together for two years, but it was a really intense two years. She taught me a whole lot of stuff I had no idea about, but we just weren't what the other person needed," Avery said, indicating that they should go into the bar which was coming up.

"After you," Avery said, holding the door open for Leila. Leila walked into the bar and smirked.

"I had half thought you'd take me into a cop bar," Leila laughed, Avery, fainting shock.

"I'm not like that," she said, leading Leila to a table towards that back of the bar. A waitress came over and took their drink order, and as she disappeared, Leila got up to take her coat off.

"So, what do you do for work?" Avery asked as Leila sat back down.

"I'm a journalist," Leila proudly said, blushing when she heard herself.

"Oh my gosh, I sound like a kid who is saying they came first in a race," she said, putting her head in her hands and laughing. Avery just looked at her and smiled lovingly.

"I thought it was cute," she said, half to herself as she sipped the Scotch, which was put down before her by the waitress.

"So, that's what I do. I work for an independent paper, and the hours are really long. That's why my ex and I broke up. We just drifted apart," Leila explained.

"How long ago was that?" Avery asked, getting the waitresses attention.

"3 months ago. We have a house together which we are selling at the moment," Leila replied, stopping as the waitress stood next to her.

"Can I order for you?" Avery asked, hoping Leila would say yes. It had been a while since she had ordered for anyone, and Leila seemed to need some taking care of.

"If you'd like," Leila replied, the delight evident on Avery's face.

"We will take the pork belly, grilled vegetables, and the mushroom and chicken gnocchi. And another round of drinks," Avery said, somewhat impressing Leila.

"I was actually going to get the gnocchi," Leila happily said, biting her bottom lip before she remembered that she was on a date.

"You don't have to pretend to be someone else. I think it's sweet that you got excited like that," Avery said, leaning forward and taking Leila's hand in hers and stroking the back of it with her thumb. Leila could feel her eyes glaze over, which meant that she was dangerously close to slipping into little space. She leaned back and caught her breath, cleared her throat, and looked around the room.

"So, is this where you bring all your dates?" Leila teased, making Avery laugh.

"Yeah, it is actually," Avery replied, shocking Leila before Avery smirked and shook her head.

"I'm joking. No, I heard that this place has an outstanding chef, and well, I like to eat good food so, I thought why not take a beautiful woman out on a date here," Avery answered, making Leila roll her eyes. The last thing she thought of herself was that she was beautiful. She almost cringed at the compliment but tried not to show that she disagreed, failing to do so.

"No? Ok, you tell me who you are then," Avery said, leaning back and folding her arms across her chest. Leila just looked around the room.

"I'm surprised we are talking with such depth," she confessed, surprised that Avery was sitting across from her, let alone wanting to know about how she saw herself.

"I don't care for small talk. I like to get into it with people, really learn who they are," Avery said, the softer side coming out once more. Leila finished her first drink just as the second round was placed on the table.

"I guess I used to be pretty. I was never as fit as you, but I also wasn't this goddamn fat," Leila said, looking down and wishing her thighs didn't touch.

"I think I would describe myself as a homebody who would rather hide from the world than be a part of it," Leila replied, more honestly than she had ever intended to be.

"Wow," Avery replied, surprised at how much Leila hated herself.

"You have been hanging around the wrong people if that's what you think about yourself," she quickly added.

"Well, I didn't think I should lie to a cop," Leila tried to joke, raising her eyebrow and looking around when Avery's face remained blank.

"Alright, you convinced me. I'll be your girlfriend," Avery suddenly said, causing Leila to choke on her drink.

"Pardon?" She asked, her eyes popping out of her head. Avery just winked at her before smiling that wicked grin.

"You are kind and gentle and compassionate, not to mention beautiful, and if you can't see that, I can't let you out of my sight. It wouldn't be right of me to let you continue to go through life hating it and yourself so much. So, I'll be your girlfriend," Avery said, pleased with herself and confident in her picking up ability.

"I don't think that's a very good reason to be with someone. I don't need you to rescue me," Leila said, somewhat annoyed that Avery had chosen her.

"I am not rescuing you," Avery replied, dragging out the word rescuing to prove a point.

"What I am doing, if you'll let me is going to show you what you are really worth. And if, after four months, you and I haven't clicked, then I will happily let you go on your way and be in your life in whatever capacity you want me in. But come on, give me a chance to give you a great time," Avery said, making Leila speechless. Leila's mouth was gaped open, but she shut it slowly as she shrugged her shoulders.

"What do I have to lose?" She said out loud, making Avery laugh as they began to have dinner.

Chapter 2

"You really do think you are God's gift to women, don't you?" Leila teased the following weekend. She and Avery had gone shopping together for outfits, which they were going to wear that night when they went out together. Avery had tried on a short red dress and was dramatically flipping her hair as she modeled it for Leila.

"Oh, I don't think it, darling, Mama knows," Avery said, winking at Leila and making her speechless for the umpteenth time that day. Leila turned and walked away as she felt her cheeks blush red, hoping that Avery missed it.

"Have you found something that you like, honey?" Avery asked, following Leila back out onto the floor.

"This isn't really my kind of store," Leila softly said, concerned that there would be nothing to fit her and feeling self-conscious.

"Can I take the lead?" Avery said, holding Leila's face in her hands. Leila looked away, shrugged her shoulders, but quickly looked back when Avery kissed the tip of her nose and melted her with her killer stare.

"Good, ok, come with me," Avery said, taking Leila's hand and began taking her around the store. Avery picked up several dresses that made Leila roll her eyes but continued to let Avery have her fun.

"None of these will look any good on me," Leila complained as Avery pushed her into a changing cubicle.

"Have you tried them on yet? Do you know that for sure, or are you just having a little tantrum because you are nervous about being in here?" Avery said, making Leila shake her head and look at herself in the mirror. She turned around, so she didn't have to see herself and undressed. Taking down the first emerald green sparkly dress, Leila turned back around and was surprised at what she saw. The dress, something that she would have never picked up in a million years, actually looked good on her.

"By the deadly silence, I'm going to take a wild guess and say that it looks nice?" Avery smugly called out, gasping as Leila opened the door. Leila was still in shock as she showed Avery the dress. The neckline showed off her full, plump breasts, their top curve looking like something from a porn magazine, the fitted waist tucked-in elegantly, and the calf to mid-thigh split showed off enough of Leila's thigh without making her feel self-conscious.

"My my, what a beautiful girl you are," Avery remarked, taking in the sight before her.

"How did you know this would look like this?!" Leila questioned, surprise and shock still evident in her voice.

"I mean, I thought it would suit you, even I couldn't predict that you would be this radiant!" Avery happily replied.

"Do you want to try on the others?" Avery asked, interested in seeing Leila in more stunning outfits. Leila tried on the other five dresses, each time being as surprised. They all made her look divine. They didn't hide the fact that she was heavier; they just complimented her. That's what Leila loved about Avery. She never made her feel like she needed to change who she was, Avery just wanted Leila to be the best version of herself that she could be in the moment.

"I can't get all of them," Leila said, holding the dresses in her arms.

"Why not?" Avery asked, frowning at her in confusion.

"Um, have you seen these price tags?" Leila laughed, putting three of the dresses back, just for Avery to pick them back up again.

"Yes. Who said anything about you buying them? I'm the one who suggested this. I'm the one who pays. Anyway, baby, I can't, in good faith, knowing how beautiful you looked in these dresses, let you leave without all of them," Avery said, adding them to the collection of outfits she had waiting for her behind the counter.

"I don't know what to say," Leila said, shocked that someone would so freely spend a couple of thousand dollars on dresses for her. Avery turned around and brought Leila in close, holding her until she felt Leila relax in her arms.

"You don't have to say anything, baby. I like doing this for you," Avery replied before turning back around and paying the woman behind the counter.

"So, I still can't believe that you did that," Leila said, happily holding onto her bags and swinging her arms. She felt different. She felt confident and secure and secretly loved the way the passers-by were looking at her designer shopping bags.

Even if this is fake confidence, gosh, it feels nice compared to the feeling of nothing I usually have, Leila thought to herself, acutely aware that the confidence stemming from an egotistical perspective wasn't the most authentic confidence to behold.

"Sweetie, this is what I am saying. Look at you, you look happy, you look free, you look like you can take on the world. If that isn't rewarding for me, I don't know what is," Avery replied, smiling and biting her bottom lip when Leila involuntarily reached out to hold her hand. Realizing what she had done, Leila freaked and tried to pull away, only to be caught by Avery's tight grip.

"Oh no, you don't. I've got you now," Avery playfully said, winking at Leila in the way, which always made Leila get butterflies in her tummy.

"Pick me up at 8?" Leila asked as they stopped outside her building. Avery wrapped her arms around Leila and stroked her hair affectionately.

"You got it, sweet thing," Avery replied before playfully slapping Leila on the ass and watching her walk into her building.

Avery then turned and walked back up the street, across the road and into a café where she sat down, ordering a coffee and watched as the people walked passed the window. She had some time to kill before she needed to go home and get ready for her date and wasn't interested in just sitting at home watching television until then. She had hoped that by now, she could bring it up with Leila.

Just take your time; you've got ages before the deadline. She might be into it. She seems like somebody who could be into it. I mean, look how cute she is, I could totally imagine her being my baby, Avery said to herself as she sipped her coffee. Avery's ex had introduced her to the MDLG world, helping her to realize her Mommy side. Avery had been so surprised the first time her ex had shown her what the kink was all about that it made her laugh. She had assumed it was the stereotypical BDSM but just getting called Mommy instead of Mistress. How wrong she had been. The problem with her ex was that she never seemed satisfied with Avery's domination. She didn't follow the rules, she challenged Avery at every turn, and nothing was ever good enough for her. At first, Avery thought it was just part of who she was as a little, but she soon grew tired of only experiencing the punishing side of their dynamic. Avery wanted more. She wanted the sweet, needy Mommy's girls that she read about. She wanted cute dates together to parks and to get pictures drawn just for her. She knew that she had to break up with her ex when she realized that she could never be the little Avery wanted and that she could never be the type of Mommy her ex needed. She just wasn't that controlling, and that's what she wanted.

"Anything else, Ma'am?" The waitress asked, interrupting Avery's thoughts. Avery looked up, somewhat startled.

"Oh, no thanks, just the check," Avery replied, checking the time and deciding that she should head home if she was going to make it on time to pick up Leila.

Leila had spent the afternoon watching cartoons. It wasn't the most productive use of her time, but if she was going to have a big night with adult drinks, adult clothes, adult conversation, she knew that she needed some little time. Usually, the weekends were when she had the most little time as the few hours she managed to get during the Monday to Friday grind was just that, only a few hours. But there was no way she was going to turn down a night with her stunning new girlfriend, even if the way they got together was the most unconventional pick up she had ever experienced. So, coming into her apartment, Leila had put her new dresses neatly in the cupboard, taken a shower, and changed into something more comfortable. Her kitten diaper and pink onesie, her hair in a messy ponytail, and her white paci. She had set herself up in front of the tv and turned on her favorite cartoons, snuggling into the pillows and blankies, imagining that it was Avery she was snuggling into.

I wonder if she'll think I'm weird, probs. I even think I'm weird, so she will as well. I wish I could be comfortable within myself, what if she finds out I want her like this, Leila thought, trying to wipe the thought from her mind. The last thing she wanted to do was push Avery away. She would usually never date somebody out of the scene, but Avery just had something that Leila loved being around. Leila couldn't put her finger on it. Avery was warm, loving, authoritarian, and tender. It made Leila ache. She was just the type of woman that Donna had been when they first got together. The thought of Donna made Leila's stomach churn. The cruel things she had said to Leila as their relationship ended haunted her. That she was ugly, too old to be a baby, that she should try to lose the weight because no one wants a big baby, that one cut her up the most. Leila shook her head as she tried to fight back the tears and buried her face in the pillows as she felt her heartbreak all over again.

"Why was she so mean?" Leila cried out loud. She sat back up and checked the time, it was 6 pm, and she knew that she should get ready so that Avery didn't walk in on her little space, but she just couldn't move. The hurt she felt inside her weighed so heavy that she closed her eyes and drifted off to sleep.

A loud knocking came from the door, startling Leila awake. It was pitch black in the room as she blinked sleepily and looked around the space.

"Leila?" Avery called from behind the door, making Leila's stomach knot.

"Oh my god," Leila said as she jumped up, turned a light on and looked around the room.

"Um, just a minute," Leila yelled out, ripping the onesie and diaper off, running into her bedroom and putting on some house clothes before racing back out to answer the door.

"Hey," Leila said, panting and pulling down her shirt. Avery looked at Leila's face and tilted her head.

"Hi," Avery replied, smirking and running her fingers through Leila's hair.

"You ready?" Avery questioned, causing Leila to snap into life and looked down at her outfit.

"Um, yeah, I am so sorry, I fell asleep," Leila said, walking backward and allowing Avery to walk inside. Avery was wearing the tight black dress with the back cut out, which she had bought earlier that day and her makeup was stunning, Leila could tell that she had taken a long time to get ready.

"Do you have kids?" Avery asked as she sat down on the couch and crossed her legs seductively. Leila looked around the living room where the cartoons were still playing. The blankies and her pacifier were still on the couch.

"Um, no, my niece was here," Leila lied, she didn't have a niece. Avery raised an eyebrow before picking up the pacifier.

"This doesn't look like a kids," she said, walking over to Leila, who froze and burned red.

"It's ok," Avery softly and affectionately said as she pushed the paci into Leila's mouth and held it there with her fingers. Leila looked into Avery's eyes fearfully, worried what she would think.

"I had my suspicions," Avery said, taking Leila's hand and gently leading her back to the couch, sitting down and positioning Leila in the nursing position. Avery wrapped her arms around Leila and stroked her cheek with her thumb.

"You had suspicions?" Leila asked, taking out her paci and slightly relaxing into Avery.

"Yeah," Avery replied, looking down on Leila lovingly.

"But I'm older than you?" Leila asked, making Avery frown.

"And? You're not older than me all the time," Avery said, winking at Leila, who giggled despite herself.

"And, I'm bigger than you," Leila said, feeling all her insecurities coming out into the open. Avery tilted her head, finally understanding the source of Leila's fears.

"Honey. Does that bother you?" Avery asked, worried that her own athletic build would be a deal-breaker.

"Doesn't it bother you? You are so beautiful, why would you want a fat baby?" Leila asked, tears forming behind her eyes. Avery gasped and shook her head.

"No, it doesn't bother me that you are who you are. Is that how you view yourself?" Avery replied, making Leila burst out crying.

"Hey, shh, it's ok," Avery cooed, soothing her.

"That's what my ex said I was," Leila said through her tears. Avery frown and sat Leila up, turning her so that she was looking her in the eye.

"Leila. Your ex sounds like a piece of shit. If she wasn't happy with you, taking it out on how you look is the weakest, most horrible thing to do, and quite frankly, she didn't deserve how amazing you are. I know we have only known each other for a week, but you are so special, and if she was too stupid to understand that, then she is just an idiot," Avery said, making Leila laugh.

"It doesn't bother me that you are older than me, and I find your body beautiful. Life is a journey, and if someone isn't willing to go on that journey with you, then they don't deserve you. I would think you were amazing if you were 50kg heavier, and I would think you were amazing if you were 15kg lighter. You're value and validity isn't determined by how much you weigh or how old you are, baby girl," Avery said, making Leila cry all over again.

"Oh honey, come here," Avery said, opening her arms and wrapping them around Leila.

"That is the nicest thing anyone has ever said to me," Leila confessed, snuggling into the crook of Avery's neck and feeling the sting of a thousand cuts ease for the first time.

"Oh, I'm sorry, I made your dress wet," Leila said, seeing that her tears had soaked a section of Avery's dress.

"You make my panties wet too," Avery said, never missing a beat and making Leila laugh.

"Really?" Leila asked, wiping her tears. Avery kissed both her cheeks before getting up.

"Really," she replied, going to the fridge.

"What do you want to drink, sweetheart? Milk, or wine? I am down for both," Avery asked, holding up the two bottles. Leila thought for a moment before smiling.

"Wine. I don't want my new dresses to go to waste," Leila replied, getting up to go and get ready.

Chapter 3

"Good morning, sleepyhead," Avery said, rolling over and brushing the hair out of Leila's face. Opening her eyes, Leila stretched and yawned before smiling at Avery.

"Hey," she softly said, her voice hoarse from the cocktails and cigarettes she had the night before.

"Hungover?" Avery asked, feeling her head begin to throb. They had both been excited to find out their kink preferences and had painted the town red, only returning back to Leila's apartment as the morning sun rose over the horizon.

"Oh, yes," Leila laughed, touching her forehead and frowning.

"Ok, we need coffee, a decent fry up, and sunglasses," Avery said, getting up and slowly making her way to the shower, turning it on and stripping. Leila followed her to the bathroom door, peeping her head around the door.

"You can come in," Avery happily said. Leila cautiously walked in, looking at Avery's fitness model body as the water trickled down her abs.

"Come and join me," Avery seductively said, making Leila blush as she was caught staring.

"Ok," Leila said, timidly taking her pajamas off and covering up her body as she got into the shower.

"How am I supposed to make sure you are clean if you are trying to hide from me?" Avery loving asked as she gently took Leila's hands away, making her blush.

"You are beautiful, Leila," Avery said, holding her face in her hands and making her look at her. Leila looked to the side, her face still in Avery's hands as Avery kissed her lips, taking her by surprise.

"I'm sorry, I thought it would be ok. We kissed last night," Avery said, letting Leila go.

"Yeah, sorry, it is. I just was surprised, I had sort of thought maybe you were only kissing me because you were drunk," Leila confessed making Avery roll her eyes.

"No, I kissed you because I wanted to. Because I find you gorgeous," Avery said, taking the bottle of shower gel in her hands and squirting it over her body before beginning to rub it in.

"Can I," Leila said, reaching out to touch Avery but stopping herself and making Avery smile.

"Yeah," Avery replied, taking Leila's hands and rubbing them over her body. She didn't need to guide Leila for very long as she took over and began rubbing her muscles and tight body passionately.

"Oh my god, your body is amazing," Leila said as she let her fingers go dangerously close to Avery's clit. Avery just bit her bottom lip and raised her eyebrow.

"What do you think you are doing?" Avery teased, making Leila giggle.

"Depends what am I allowed to do," Leila replied, surprised at how confident she now felt.

Avery leaned against the shower wall, took Leila by the wrist, and washed her hand clean of any shower gel before placing it against her pussy, pushing Leila's fingers passed her slit, opening up her pussy lips.

"I'll let you do that," Avery whispered, Leila, enjoying the feel of Avery's body. Gently, running her fingers up and down Avery's pussy, pressing into her cunt, watching as Avery shook her head.

"Not today," Avery replied, Leila, wanting a reason but accepting the boundary and going back to stroking her.

"Tell me where I can touch you," Avery said, gasping as Leila began to tease her clit.

"Wherever you want," Leila said, shrugging her shoulder, half worried that Avery wouldn't want to touch her at all.

"Well then," Avery said, taking Leila's hand from her cunt and turning her around so that she was facing the wall. Avery took Leila's hands and put them high up against the wall making her giggle.

"You're not meant to laugh when I frisk you," Avery playfully said, beginning to massage down Leila's body sensually. Leila hadn't been touch like this in years and felt her head spin as she felt Avery snake her hands over her shoulders and breasts, coming around to the back of her and kissing down to her ass.

"My god, you are divine," Avery mumbled to herself as she grabbed Leila's ass in both hands and grinded against her, feeling her clit harden. Leila felt hers do the same and gasped as she felt Avery's kisses going further over her ass. Turning her around, Avery was kneeling before her, raised an eyebrow, and gently patted Leila's thigh.

"Leg up, baby girl," Avery said, watching as Leila put her foot on the edge of the shower ledge.

"Just tell me to stop if you don't want this anymore," Avery said as she stuck her tongue out and slowly licked Leila's slit, making her shiver and her nipples harden.

"Oh, I knew you would be a sweet girl," Avery said, burying her face between Leila's thighs and eating her out passionately. Leila gasped and moaned, feeling Avery's tongue inside of her, making her wonder how she could get it so deep.

"Play with your tits for me," Avery said, coming up for air, just to dive back in, Leila obeying her instruction immediately. Leila pushed herself onto Avery's face, moaning as the water sprinkled their bodies.

"Fuck," Leila said, almost swearing she could feel Avery smile as she continued to suck her clit and curl her fingers inside of her, only easing off to allow her tongue to take over. Leila shuddered and buckled over, grabbing Avery's head and pressing it against her as she felt the earth-shattering orgasm rage through her body. Avery tapped the side of Leila's thigh, causing her to let her head go and she came up, gasping for air.

"Fuck me that was hot," Avery said, Leila, sliding down the wall and making Avery smile and join her.

"I loved that little bit of suffocation play you had going at the end. I didn't know I was into that,"

Avery said, wiping her chin and letting the water pour over her face, slicking her hair back.

"I didn't mean it, it was just so good I didn't want it to end," Leila quietly said, making Avery laugh.

"I'm glad you liked it. The first time can sometimes be really awkward," Avery replied, seeing Leila's face and shaking her head.

"No, that was not awkward," Avery said, cracking her neck before getting up, reaching out her hand to Leila.

"I've just eaten, but you need breakfast," Avery said, Leila, taking her hand and standing up.

"Cringe," Leila said, making Avery laugh and gently spank her ass as she walked out of the shower first.

"I'll just get the salad," Leila said as she folded the menu back up and took a sip from her glass of water. Avery looked over her menu, Leila's sad face telling her all that she needed to know.

"Do you want a salad? Because that face is

not the face of someone happy about their selection," Avery said.

"I just think I should get it," Leila said, shrugging her shoulder.

"Ok, forget about what you think you should or shouldn't get. What would you want to get if you could have anything off the menu?" Avery asked, Leila, opening up the menu once more and looking over the choices.

"A burger and fries with a chocolate shake," Leila said in almost no time at all.

"Right, then baby, that's what you should get," Avery said, reaching out and holding Leila's hand.

"But, it's not the most healthy choice," Leila said, looking around at the other patrons.

"People look at me like I shouldn't be eating that sort of stuff when they see me," Leila said, looking into her lap. Avery got up and moved so that she was sitting next to her and wrapped her arm around her.

"And if anybody looks at you like you

shouldn't be doing exactly what you want, I'm going to have words with them," Avery said, taking Leila's head and resting it on her shoulder.

"I'm not going to let anyone hurt you, sweet girl," Avery said, making Leila's heart swell.

"I really like you," Leila whispered, feeling Avery's body against hers.

"I really like you too," Avery replied, winking at Leila.

Chapter 4

Avery was a dream come true. She was kind, considerate, and never seemed to push Leila too far out of her comfort zone, but just enough that she started to feel brave again. It showed in her work too. Her articles had taken on a flare she had thought she had lost, even her skin seemed to glow.

"It's all thanks to you, you know," Leila said over late lunch. Avery was tired. Leila could see by the sleepy smile that she gave her as she read Leila's latest article.

"Well, I can't take all the credit," Avery replied. Avery had scratched up knuckles from a bar fight she had been called to last night, Leila only seeing her now, the first time in three days.

"It looks like they are getting infected," Leila said, frowning as she looked at Avery's hands.

"They'll be fine," Avery said, playfully rolling her eyes at Leila.

"Come on, come back home with me and let me dress them properly. Let me look after you," Leila said, standing up and waiting for Avery to join her.

"Shouldn't it be the other way around?" Avery said, slowly standing and walking over to join her.

"Not all the time," Leila said, her smile warming Avery's heart.

Leila opened the door to her apartment, the afternoon sun making the crystals on her television cabinet glisten and shine.

"Sit down," Leila said, going over to her medicine box and took out the supplies.

"Want a drink?" Leila asked, making Avery laugh.

"It's 3 in the afternoon," Avery replied Leila, coming to the couch with her medicine box and beginning to lay out everything she needed.

"Yes, and?" Leila questioned, making Avery laugh.

"No, I don't, but when you've been such a good girl and looked after Mommy, how about I reward you?" Avery said, causing Leila's head to tilt.

"Reward?" Leila asked, wanting to know more details. Avery just sat back and held her hand out to Leila, who began disinfecting the cuts.

"Ouch," Avery plainly said, trying not to flinch.

"Sorry," Leila replied, wrapping Avery's hands in bandages and sitting back.

"You know how we went dress shopping, and it was enjoyable, to say the least?" Avery asked, reminding Leila of the first time she had trusted Avery.

"Yeah," Leila cautiously replied, not sure where Avery was talking the conversation.

"Well, I wonder if you would want to go, little shopping?" Avery asked, Leila, rolling her eyes.

"Of course, I would!" Leila exclaimed, clapping her hands.

"Great. I was actually nervous that you might say no," Avery confessed, making Leila laugh.

"Um, why?" Leila questioned. It was very rare that Leila saw Avery nervous, but she liked it. It made her feel special, that Avery was just as afraid to lose her as she was Avery.

"I don't know. Everyone is different, and I kinda assumed you'd love it, but at the same time, you make me nervous. I don't want you to think I am trying to buy your affection or love or whatever," Avery said, making Leila laugh.

"I don't, don't worry," Leila replied, snuggling into Avery and closing her eyes as she felt Avery's arms close around her.

"I could just fall asleep right here," Leila softly said, feeling Avery kiss her forehead.

"But then we couldn't go shopping," Avery said.

"Oh, you mean right now?" Leila replied,

sitting up and looking at Avery.

"Yeah. There's an event tonight, and I know there will be a few vendors. We could always go online, but when there is an opportunity to feel and try on the product, I like to take that opportunity," Avery explained. Leila smiled at her before silently standing up and taking the medicine box back to the kitchen.

"What is it?" Avery asked, seeing something in Leila's face that she couldn't figure out.

"Nothing. It's just, I didn't know it could feel this nice," Leila said, feeling tears well in her eyes. She liked that Avery didn't try to comfort her and let her feel her feelings instead of trying to make everything ok.

"Are you alright with it feeling this good?" Avery asked. Leila thought about the question shaking her head and shrugging her shoulders.

"I want to be," she said, making it sound more like a question than a statement of conviction.

"But?" Avery asked, giving Leila time to

understand her own thoughts.

"But I'm not, and it might be like this for a while, and I want to be transparent with you because I don't want you to think I'm awful or ungrateful because I'm not. I just, it hurts every time you are so nice to me because, for the longest time, I was told that I didn't deserve nice things or for nice things to happen to me. I guess at some point, I started to believe that was true as well, and it'll just take a minute for that to undo," Leila explained, looking plainly at Avery once she finished talking. Avery stood in front of her and slowly nodded her head.

"You don't scare me," she whispered before winking and taking Leila's hand in hers.

"I'm glad," Leila replied, grabbing her keys and walking out the door.

Avery and Leila caught a taxi to the event, arriving an hour after it had started.

"Do you think it's a problem?" Leila nervously asked, making Avery smile.

"It's not a sit-down dinner. Nobody cares when or actually if we even show up, so yes, it is totally fine," Avery replied, making Leila laugh. They walked into the bar, and Avery loved that Leila immediately held her hand.

"Oh, do all the cute things make my baby girl feel little," Avery whispered in Leila's ear. She knew that there was no need for discretion, but she enjoyed turning Leila into the shy little girl she had come to love.

"Mommy," Leila whined, turning red. Avery loved that about Leila. She triggered so easily.

The event was held in a large conference hall in the middle of the city. Avery had been to many of the events held in this room, and she knew the view over the park was breathtaking. Tonight, however, the blinds pulled down on the windows and for a good reason. This event, while not particularly exclusive, still attracted all manner of clientele from all industries, and discretion was more than welcomed. As they moved around the room, they saw a large area set up for play, including a ball pit and painting station. Diaper, onesie, and pacifier vendors were set up along the far wall, and a QandA stage was set up in the middle of the room.

"This is really cool. How did you know about this?" Leila asked, looking around the room, smiling widely.

"Mommy's just clever," Avery replied, taking Leila's hand and leading her over to the multiple onesie vendors.

"What about this one?" Avery asked, Leila, looking at her like she had lost her mind.

"Alright," Avery laughed, putting the space-themed onesie down.

"This is more what I am going for," Leila said, holding up the cute black and white ghost onesie.

"Oh, wow, I can imagine you in this!" Avery exclaimed, taking it from Leila's hands and looking for more styles with a similar flare.

After half an hour, Avery held a bag full of onesies in one hand and Leila's hand in the other, getting slightly pulled as they made their way to the painting wall.

"You can do one painting baby girl, but then we have to go home," Avery said, causing Leila to take as long as she could get away with to make her creation. Clocking onto Leila's sneaky ways after 20minutes, Avery told Leila that she would have to finish the painting at home, causing Leila to give her puppy dog eyes and pout.

"Don't give me that, Mommy was clear," Avery said, Leila, realizing that it was better to be a good girl than a brat, and stood up reluctantly, pleasing Avery. There was something in the way that Leila submitted that drove Avery wild. It was more than just her following an instruction. It was her willingness to be inconvenienced for Avery's desires. Avery knew that she could push Leila to do whatever it was that she wanted, and her need to directed turned Avery on unlike anything she had ever experienced.

Is it that? Or is it the power and responsibility that comes with it? Avery thought as she looked over to Leila, who was happily walking next to her. Deciding that it didn't matter what the reason was, that the feeling was reward enough, Avery stopped walking and turned Leila into her.

"I love you," Avery suddenly said to Leila, who froze. She hadn't heard those words, said with such conviction in years, and the sound made her mind spin.

"Why?" Leila softly asked, looking down and kicking the sidewalk. Avery let her eyes smile as she reached out to slowly lift Leila's chin to make her look at her dead in the eye.

"What's not to love?" Avery replied, making Leila's eyes glaze over, and her mouth gape open in surprise.

"I know that sometimes you don't feel loveable. But I love you, and nothing that you are about to say or do will change that," Avery said, making Leila laugh despite herself and shake her head.

"You don't have to say it back. I just wanted you to know where I was at," Avery said, as they began to walk down the street once more. Leila was glad that Avery didn't want a reply because she didn't have one. It had been so long since Leila had felt the type of feelings that Avery seemed to reach so easily, it felt almost too good to be true, and the fear that it could all go away stopped Leila from diving as deeply as Avery.

Conflicted, Leila kissed Avery goodnight and closed her door, looking around her apartment and going straight to the kitchen and pouring herself a drink. She took out her phone and looked through the photos she had taken with Avery, hating herself for not being able to give Avery the easy, happy relationship she wished she could.

Why does it have to be so hard for you?! Leila felt her heart cry out as she had a shower, the hot water pouring over her body, and her alcohol-filled veins making her head spin. Deciding to sit down on the shower floor, she put her head in her hands and began to cry. It wasn't that Avery had said that she loved her; it was the pain that Donna didn't. It wasn't that Avery had bought her things, it was that Leila wanted it to be Donna who did. It wasn't about Avery at all. It was about Donna. It was that Avery was everything Donna wasn't, and it was that Leila wanted it to be Donna. Shaking her head, wondering why she still grieved for that soulless, cruel woman, Leila stood up and put her face to the showerhead and let the water wash her tears away.

Maybe I don't know that I am allowed to be happy or something, Leila thought, deciding that drinking in the shower was a terrible idea and that she needed to see a therapist before she ruined everything with Avery.

Chapter 5

Leila had found a therapist online who had a practice close to where she lived and thought that she might as well give it a go.

What do I have to lose? Leila thought to herself as she crossed the road and picked up a take away coffee before continuing down the street. She walked up the concrete stairs, opened the glass door, and walked inside the small foyer, the receptionist greeting her warmly.

"Hey there," she said, smiling at Leila.

"Hi, I have an appointment with Christina Clarke," Leila replied, putting her hands in her pockets.

"Leila? Great, go right in," the receptionist said, and she pointed to the hallway. Leila gave her one of those, smiles that are more like pushing your lips together and walked down the hall.

"Hi, Leila?" Christina warmly said, stopping

Leila in her tracks. Leila had seen this woman before. At the event her and Avery had been too only a few nights ago, this woman was one of the guests on the QandA panel. The woman didn't seem to recognize her, though, but it would become apparent soon enough that they shared similar interests.

"Yeah, hi," Leila said, sitting on the chair Christina directed her to. Due to Christina had been one of the guest speakers on the QandA, Leila already knew that she was a Mommy, but she incorporated a fair bit of extreme S and M into her and her subs sex lives. It wasn't something Leila was particularly into, but she appreciated the diversity of the speakers of that night.

"So, what brings you here?" Christina asked, crossing her legs and waiting for Leila. Leila sipped her coffee, looked to the side, and sighed.

"I think I'm addicted to pain. Like the emotional kind, and it doesn't feel good," Leila said, Christina, nodding and writing on her tablet.

"What makes you say that?" She

questioned. Leila was glad she was allowed to elaborate.

"I'm dating this girl. She is amazing, everything that anybody could want, gives me the freedom to be myself, speaks my love language, is gorgeous, but I feel conflicted about her love. Like, I want to reject it, but I have no reason to," Leila said Christina listening.

"Have you felt this way in other relationships?" Christina asked, Leila, biting her bottom lip.

"No, my last relationship was for six years, she was older than I was, she changed when I wasn't what she wanted anymore and made me feel like shit," Leila said, happy that she didn't feel the need to cry.

"If she made you feel like shit, and this new woman you are with doesn't, I wonder if you still feel like shit. Maybe you don't feel like you deserve to be loved by this new woman because you haven't healed from your past relationship," Christina said, offering Leila a thought she hadn't contemplated before.

"Yeah, maybe," Leila said, sighing.

"Well, how do I get over my ex? Why am I still feeling this way when she was so cruel?" Leila asked. Christina nodded her head.

"Sometimes, when people treat us in alignment with how we feel about ourselves, the desire to be reminded of that is strong. Tell me something you would never do, something really out there," Christina said, Leila, thinking hard, trying to take in her words.

"I'd never want to go skydiving," Leila finally said.

"Ok. So now imagine that you are with somebody who is an adrenaline junkie and goes skydiving with their mates, has a whole network of friends from skydiving, and constantly reminds you that you should try it. They could be beautiful, funny, speak your love language and be the best person in the world, but they go against one of your big values, which in this case could be safety. You see, when somebody displays behaviors that are against who and what we think we are, we reject them, and those who are in alignment with us, and we accept them. So, if you think you are nothing, and somebody treats you like you are something, do you see how that is in conflict? So what we need to do, is get you seeing yourself in a better light because you know it's not right to be treated like trash," Christina said, causing Leila to burst into tears. For the first time in her life, she had an explanation as to why she allowed people to be horrible to her, and a lifetime of bullying experiences came crashing down on her.

"Here," Christina said, offering her a box of tissues.

"It's totally normal to cry, that's why you come here, to heal yourself. It takes guts. You should be really proud of yourself," Christina said, making Leila cry harder.

The way home was a blur, mostly because Leila still had tears in her eyes, which refused to leave, but she was also filled with new thoughts and feelings. She was surprised that one session could have that effect on her, but she was most surprised as to why it had taken her so long.

"It was so great. She really got me and knew what to say," Leila said to Avery on the phone that night. Avery was working but had taken five minutes to check in on Leila.

"I'm so happy for you, honey," Avery replied. She was a big advocate for seeking help for any and all parts of life.

"I told you it was like going to the gym but for your mind," Avery said, making Leila laugh.

"I guess Mommy is always right," Leila laughed, snuggling into bed.

"Not all the time, but mostly. So, are you seeing her again?" Avery asked, hoping that Leila had booked another appointment.

"Yeah, I'm going to see her weekly," Leila replied, making Avery smile.

"Good girl," Avery said, looking around. She was leaning against a street light waiting for her partner to collect their dinner order.

"Well, Mommy has to go now, baby girl. Are we still on for tomorrow?" Avery said, seeing him walk out of the store.

"Yes, I'm really looking forward to it, Mommy," Leila replied, snuggling into the shirt Avery had left behind. She had deliberately bought a large shirt to wear to bed so that she could spray it with her perfume and leave it for Leila to find. She wanted Leila to be able to wear it around the house if she wished, and the thought of that made Avery smile.

"What are you wearing?" Avery suddenly asked, her partner raising his eyebrows and giving her a smile before sitting back in the car.

"Your shirt Mommy," Leila happily said, throwing her arms in the air as she said it, wishing that Avery was there with her to cuddle her at that moment.

"Good girl," Avery replied, before hanging up the phone.

"Don't look at me like that, you'd asked the same question if anyone wanted you around for long enough," Avery said, teasing her partner before driving back out onto the road.

"Is it too much?" Leila asked. Avery turned around to see her baby girl standing in front of her. Leila was wearing a diaper, her new ghost onesie, and her hair out. Avery found herself speechless for the first time.

"No, you look, amazing," Avery breathlessly said, making Leila smile and look down at her feet. Finding that she believed Avery for the smallest moments, she smiled again, happy that she was beginning to change her thoughts about herself. Not the surface layer thoughts, but those deep subconscious ones.

"But you need some sockies, baby girl," Avery said, taking Leila's hand and walking her back into the bedroom and sitting her on the bed.

"I think the pink ones are going to go really nicely," Avery said, taking them out of the cupboard and walking back over to Leila.

"No, Mommy," Leila said, kicking her feet so

that Avery couldn't get them on her feet.

"Oi. Don't test me, little one," Avery sternly said, grabbing Leila's chin in her hand and making her look Avery in the eye.

"But I don't want those Mommy," Leila said, pouting.

"I think somebody needs Mommy to teach them a lesson," Avery said, putting the socks on the bed and swiftly turning Leila onto her tummy.

"Stay," Avery commanded. She thought back to the types of punishments that Leila said would be ok and decided to combine two of them.

"Do you know what happens to naughty girls?" Avery asked, planning out her punishment as she traced her fingertips over Leila's skin.

"Answer me," she angrily said, raising her voice and bringing both hands down on Leila's ass, making her squirm.

"No Mommy, what happens," Leila said, feeling the sting through her diaper, surprising her.

"They don't just get punished, they get

corrected," Avery explained, grabbing Leila's thighs and squeezing them until she heard Leila gasp in pain.

"So, Mommy is going to remind you to be a good girl. And I don't think you're going to forget this for a very, very long time," Avery said, whispering the second half of the sentence. Leila shivered. She could tell that Avery was enjoying this, and as she was rolled onto her back, she knew that Avery meant business.

"I don't think you understand how much it hurts Mommy when you are rude," Avery said as she got on top of Leila and straddled her, holding her down with one hand between her breasts and one on the leather strap. She spoke slowly as she flogged Leila's thighs time after time.

"Mommy," Leila gasped, surprised at how strong Avery was.

"Try again. The only thing I want to hear from that pretty little mouth is, I'm sorry, Mommy," Avery said as she switched hands and began flogging Leila's other exposed thigh making her squirm.

"Oh, you think this is debatable? Do you think we are having a negotiation, baby doll?" Avery said as she moved her hand onto Leila's neck.

"No, Mommy," Leila said, seeing that she was making Avery angry.

"Now, you are deliberately ignoring Mommy?" Avery said, dropping the strap and slapping Leila across the face.

"I'm sorry, Mommy," Leila loudly said, Avery, smirking.

"There we go, that's better," Avery said, slapping Leila two more times.

"Next time, don't make me ask twice," Avery said, getting off Leila and grabbing her wrist, pulling her down the hall and bending her over the back of the couch.

"Spread your fucking legs," Avery growled, waiting for Leila to obey her instruction.

"I told you that you'd remember this," Avery said, taking a vibrating dildo and lubing it before pulling Leila's diaper aside and pushing it into her ass.

"Oh, baby girl, did you think Mommy was going to put it in your pussy?" Avery teased, watching as Leila's body reacted.

"Let me feel those nipples," Avery said, reaching around Leila and rubbing her nipples, pinching them and enjoying how hard they were.

"Don't worry, your pussy isn't going to be ignored," Avery said, taking a thicker vibrator and pushing it into Leila, who whimpered and bent her head forward. Avery knew that she was close to her psychological limit and decided to soften the punishment to extend the time Leila could take it for.

"Put your hands behind your head, baby girl," Avery loving whispered into Leila's ear, running her fingertips over her body and giving her goosebumps.

"I'm sorry, Mommy," Leila said, tears running down her cheeks as Avery turned her around.

"I know you are, baby girl. But Mommy isn't done with you yet," Avery said, fastening a strap on to her waist and sitting on a chair.

"Get on your knees," Avery affectionately said, beckoning Leila with a finger, her other hand rubbing the cock between her thighs.

"Open wide baby girl," Avery said, pushing her hips forward and wrapping her hand through Leila's hair and pushing her cock into Leila's mouth, watching as she began to jerk her head up and down.

"That's it," Avery said. She had always thought it fascinating how this turned her on. It was such a simple act, but for some reason, it made her clit throb and her pussy drip.

"Get up," Avery said, pulling Leila off her only to pull out the vibrator in Leila's pussy and replace it with her cock, making Leila sit on her lap, facing her.

"Bounce for Mommy, let me see those titties shake," Avery said. She could see that she was pushing Leila, but she smiled at her as Leila rode her, seeing Leila want to please her.

"Such a good girl. You were so good taking your punishment, you can cum when you want baby girl, Mommy wants to treat her little one," Avery said, seeing the change in Leila's face, knowing that her punishment was over and gasped as she felt Leila push her back as she fucked herself on top of Avery.

"That's it, take what you want, get what you need little one," Avery said as she felt Leila tense up and shudder as she came, holding her as she came down and crashed into sub drop.

"Mommy's got you," Avery reassuring said over and over, and she gently took her cock from Leila's body and took it off. She took out the vibrator from her ass and repositioned the diaper and onesie comfortably on Leila.

"Mommy," Leila whined, reaching out for Avery, who came to the couch and laid on top of her.

"Mommy's here. Mommy's protecting you," Avery gently said, as Leila grabbed at her like a cat flexing its paws on a carpet.

"I feel weird," Leila said, holding onto Avery.

"I know you do, and it's ok to feel this. You've never felt this way after a punishment before?" Avery asked, kissing all over Leila's face and making her smile.

"No, never," Leila said, shaking her head. Avery brushed the hair out of her eyes and got off Leila, sitting up and watching as Leila also sat up.

"It can happen, it's called sub drop. It's like when you crash after a scene. It's totally normal. You don't have to think so much into it. There's nothing wrong with you because you feel a little down. What is something you think might make you feel better?" Avery said. Leila wasn't sure what she wanted to do. She felt as though she just wanted to escape.

"Could we just go for a drive and listen to music?" Leila asked as she wiped a tear away from her eye.

"Yeah, baby girl, come on," Avery replied,

taking Leila's hand and leading her into the bedroom to get changed.

Chapter 6

They drove around the city for what felt like forever. Leila rested her head against the window and listened to her playlist while Avery drove and gently stroked her thigh.

"Have you ever wanted just to run away from all of this?" Leila asked, looking out the window at the concrete jungle.

"Have you spoken to your therapist about how you feel as well?" Avery asked, turning into a side street and parking the car. She took off hers and Leila's seatbelts and turned to face Leila.

"No, not really. We just talk about how I feel about myself," Leila replied. Avery saw the look on Leila's face and knew that if Leila decided to run away and out of this city, that she wouldn't be able to catch up with her. It wasn't as easy for Avery to leave the city, and she hoped that she could somehow make Leila want to stay.

"I don't know what to tell you," Avery said, sighing and reaching her hand out to Leila.

"I don't either. I want to feel happy, but I just can't seem to. And I don't know if that's because of me, my past or the way I deal with stuff. It just seems too easy for everyone else but me," Leila said, putting her seat down and looking up the car ceiling. Avery did the same, and as they lay looking up at the ceiling, they held hands, both seeming to know that the journey they were both on was about to change.

Leila put the last of her things in the trunk of her car, Avery watching as she leaned against the brick wall of the apartment building. They had spent the last few days together, Leila deciding that she needed to get out of the city and clear her head. Avery wishing that she could stop her, but knowing that it would be selfish as this is what Leila needed and wanted. They had had one last Mommy and little interaction, and Avery tried to fight back her tears as Leila closed the trunk and turned around.

"Jesus," Avery said, shaking her head, looking up at the perfect blue sky and wiping her tears.

"I'm sorry, Avery. I wish that this could have been different," Leila said, unsure if she was allowed to hold Avery, Avery reaching out and pulling her into her and holding her like she would die if she let go.

"I know," Avery whispered, crying silent tears as she pushed Leila away and crossed her arms across her chest, nodding her head.

"You better go, baby girl," Avery said, looking into her arms and feeling her heartbreak.

"I'll message you when I know where I am going," Leila said, getting into the car and driving away.

"Fuck," Avery said to herself as she turned and walked away, feeling her heart being ripped out and left on that sidewalk.

Avery went to the store and bought three bottles

of bourbon on her way home. Calling in sick for her shift, she threw her phone against the wall, shattering the screen. She stripped down to her lingerie and opened the first bottle, drinking from it and playing music on the loudest level on her headphones. Sitting on the couch, drinking, crying, throwing the pillows against the wall was how she spent the rest of her day.

Fuck this shit, she thought to herself, halfway through her second bottle. She was somewhat surprised that she was still conscious, although she wondered how much of the night she would remember by the morning. Taking a shower, she put on the first thing she could find and headed out.

As she walked down the street, she wasn't sure what she was feeling, or even if she was feeling at all, she just needed to walk.

This is fucked, absolutely fucking fucked, she thought. Deciding to walk through a park to try and calm her mind, Avery thought back over the woman she had been in relationships with in the past. She didn't remember a woman getting under her skin like this before. She felt as though something had been taken from her, something that she had to willingly let go of because if she didn't, she would only be hurting Leila more, and that was something she couldn't imagine doing. She sat down on a park bench, the feeling of emptiness in her heart seeming to seep to the other parts of her, and as she lay down on the bench, she curled her legs up to her chest and closed her eyes.

"Hi, can I check-in for three nights please," Leila said to the receptionist of the motel. After getting the room key, Leila drove to the room, opened the door, and dropped her bag. It was nothing special, but it would do just fine until she figured out where she was going. Leila took a shower, put on her pajamas, and lay on the bed. Taking out her phone, she messaged Avery, delighted when Avery called her almost immediately.

"Hey baby," Avery said. Leila could tell that she had been drinking but could still hear the pain in her voice.

"Hi. So I'm in a motel-like 7 hours out of the city. I think I might keep driving in a few days and stop at a small country town another 8 hours from here," Leila said, snuggling into Avery's shirt. Leila heard Avery sniff and then sigh.

"Ok. I am really happy that you are doing this, it's important that you find who you really are and stuff," Avery said, sitting up on the bench and wiping her tears.

"Are you drunk?" Leila said, half laughing, making Avery laugh.

"Yeah, I am. I'm dealing with this in probably the most useless way, but hey. Don't judge me please," Avery said, worried that Leila would think she was pathetic.

"No! No judgment at all, Mommy," Leila said, making Avery burst into tears as she heard her say, Mommy.

"Sorry, maybe I shouldn't call you that

anymore?" Leila asked, not wanting to make this any harder on Avery than it clearly already was for her.

"No, I kinda like it. You can still call me Mommy," Avery replied, making Leila bite her bottom lip.

"But, baby girl, Mommy has to go and get home. I've just realized how dark it is," Avery said, sobering up enough to realize that she had put herself in a dangerous situation.

"Are you out?" Leila asked, wondering if Avery was with another girl.

"Yeah, I went for a walk. I needed some air," Avery replied, making Leila smile and rollover.

"Ok, goodnight then," Avery said, holding her breath and beginning to walk out of the park.

"Night, Mommy," Leila said, Avery quickly ending the phone call and bursting back into tears as she left the park.

Chapter 7

The hangover that greeted Avery when she woke the next day was unlike anything she had experienced, and as she raced for the bathroom, she knew that she had ruined bourbon for herself forever.

"Goddamn it," Avery said out loud between being sick. When she did finally empty the contents of her stomach, she took a shower and headed out to get breakfast. She put her headphones on and walked down the street, angrily looking at every pretty face which passed her. Avery had the type of look which made other gay women instantly interested, and for the first time in her life, she cursed herself for being so alluring. She didn't want them looking at her. She wanted Leila. Leila with her beautiful face and soft lips. Her baby girl with the body of a goddess, her soft and creamy skin always warm to touch. Avery rolled her eyes to herself as she thought about Leila as she crossed the road and walked into a café. The smell of burned toast hit her instantly, and she sat down at the closest free table. Ordering a black coffee and a full breakfast, Avery sighed as she opened her phone, deciding that she needed to buy a new one.

Maybe having a giant tantrum wasn't the smartest thing to do, she thought to herself, reflecting on last night's decisions, making herself laugh despite herself. She reached for the sugar packets and taking one out, ripped it open with her teeth before pouring it into her coffee and stirring. She wanted to message Leila, wanted to tell her that she was coming with her, that she was giving up her life in the city and that they would be together once again but decided to leave her phone in her pocket.

That would be the most selfish thing you could do, you know that she needs time and space to figure some stuff out, Avery thought as she looked at a happy couple passing her table, giggling intimately with each other.

Well, this just sucks, she thought, sighing and wondering how fast this day could pass.

Leila had spent her time sitting in her motel room thinking. She made tea after tea and thought. Thought about all the things Donna had done and said to her, thought about what her therapist had told her, and thought about Avery.

She was like my knight in shining armor, but I guess I need to save myself, Leila thought to herself as she made her fifth tea for the morning. It wasn't like Leila to cut and run, she wished that she had done this to Donna and not to Avery, but as she thought more and more about it, she was glad that she did it nonetheless.

"It wasn't that Avery was bad, but she gave me so many experiences that I wasn't ready for. I wasn't ready for the intense love and passion she gave me," Leila said out loud. Somehow, hearing her own thoughts made it easier to comprehend what her head was doing.

"So, a little bit of separation will be good, because I can have a moment to learn to love myself first and then when I go back to Avery, if she has me back, then I won't be freaked out every time she does something nice," Leila said, continuing to think out loud. She sighed and opened the door of the motel room. She was meant to check out today, but she wasn't sure if she even wanted to go on.

"I don't think I have to go that far just to be ok with being liked," Leila said to the birds who were jumping around in the gutter. She finished her tea and went inside, grabbed her bags, and put them in the car. Sitting in the parking lot and deciding what to do, either turn around and go back home or continue and see what other personal revelations she could discover. She thought about Avery, the perfect woman that she chanced upon at an imperfect time.

"Typical," Leila thought as she rolled her eyes to herself and turned on the ignition. Driving out of the lot, she hit the road, turning on a playlist

Avery made her and began driving the 8 hours to the next town.

"Hi, I'm glad I could reach you," Leila said, calling Avery. It was the middle of the night, but Leila knew Avery would be awake.

"Of course, how's it all going?" Avery replied. She got up from where she was sitting and walked outside, the night air hitting her like a slap in the face.

"Pretty good. I have almost reached that town. I'm about an hour away from the border. I think I'll stay there for a week and then decided what I'm doing next. If I stay there or if I come back," Leila said, Avery just nodded her head silently.

"You sound happier," Avery finally said, making Leila smile.

"I am actually. I even ate a burger in public today," Leila said.

"Wow, solid progress!" Avery laughed, happy that Leila was beginning to feel comfortable in her own skin. Silence fell between the two of them, the empty feeling in Avery's stomach, making her sigh.

"I miss you," Avery said, wishing there had been some way she could have kept Leila with her.

"I miss you too, I still sleep with your shirt," Leila said, hoping that it would make Avery understand how deeply she still felt about her.

"Do you? That's really cute, send me a photo if you've got time. I'd love to see," Avery replied, imaging Leila lying in bed with her shirt on.

"If you're lucky," Leila teased, making Avery laugh.

"I have to go, babe. Thanks for calling me," Avery said, wishing that she was at home so she could burst into tears.

"Ok, talk to you soon," Leila replied, hanging up the phone and closing her eyes shut, trying not to let the tears escape her eyes.

Chapter 8

The weeks passed painfully slowly, Leila deciding that she would stay in town for a while and finding a furnished studio apartment. Avery went through the motions of work, house jobs, and sleep. She had been tasked with a new partner, a rookie straight out of the academy, and she felt like those grumpy old guys who had trained her.

"Hey, hey, what's up," Bec joyfully said when she saw Avery waiting by the car. They were to patrol in the car today, and Avery had to get Bec acquainted with the streets.

"Nothing, get in," Avery plainly said, annoyed by how bubbly the girl was.

"You got up on the wrong side of the bed today," Bec muttered as she sat down, Avery just looked at her before rolling her eyes and driving onto the road. All she wanted to do was drive to Leila, not have this rookie with the enthusiasm of a puppy coming for a ride-along.

"So, what sort of stuff are you into?" Bec asked, looking out the window.

"None of your fucking business," Avery replied, smiling, feeling somewhat satisfied that she seemed to crush Bec's spirt.

"Geez, you're a hardass," Bec sighed, shaking her head.

"My girlfriend and I are on a weird thing where she has gone to find herself," Avery said, deciding that if she was going to have to spend the day with this kid, then she might as well try to be friendly.

"Rough, no wonder you are so grumpy," Bec replied, making Avery scoff.

"Hey. So, what about you?" Avery asked. She wished that she hadn't the moment she saw Bec's eyes light up and then proceeded to tell Avery every little thing about herself. Where she went to school, where she worked before becoming a police officer, how she and her boyfriend wanted to buy a dog.

Well, this was a mistake, Avery thought to herself as she looked at the time wishing Bec would shut up.

"How was your day?" Avery asked Leila, ringing her the moment she got home from work.

"Fine. I think that I'll come back in about a week or so. I've had a lot of time to think, and I feel like, if you are keen, then I would like to be with you again," Leila said, holding her breath. Avery didn't know what to say. This is what she had been waiting for for over a month, and now that Leila was finally saying the words she wanted to hear, she felt numb.

"Will I still be enough for you?" Avery asked, feeling worried that Leila would want something she couldn't give her.

"Mommy, you were always enough," Leila said, making Avery burst into tears.

"Oh my god, baby," Avery said, wiping them away and pacing around her apartment.

"Avery?" Leila asked, unsure of how Avery

was feeling.

"Yeah, it's ok, I'm fine. I'm more than fine. I thought that you wouldn't want to be with me when you came back, even if you were coming back," Avery said, making Leila realize for the first time how hard it had been on Avery.

"I am so sorry. I didn't realize that this was hurting you so much," Leila said, wishing she could get in the car right now and drive until she reached Avery.

"I didn't want you to know. I wanted you to have the time you needed to sort out all the stuff you wanted to sort out, and then, well, I didn't really have a plan after that. Making sure you had the time to clear your head and stuff was my only priority," Avery said, making Leila beam.

"You really are the best person I have ever known, let alone been with. I'll take two days to get back home, but I'm ok now. Mommy? I'm coming home," Leila said, hanging up the phone and smiling up at the ceiling. She didn't hurt anymore. She could still identify the hurt, but when she thought about the things which haunted her, they didn't cause her the unwavering pain and heartache they had in the past.

"I got one thing right," Leila said, putting on Avery's shirt and falling asleep.

Avery felt like a madwoman as she raced around to all of the shops she knew Leila loved. Picking up flowers, chocolates, a necklace, and books, Avery knew that she didn't have much time left before Leila got back into town. They had arranged to meet at Avery's apartment, Avery said that Leila could sleep there until she found a place of her own, but was secretly hoping that she would never want to leave. Avery went to the liquor store and bought Leila's favorite wine and then dropped into the donut shop and bought a dozen glazed donuts before returning home. She washed her sheets, vacuumed the place and cleaned the bathroom, putting the flowers in a vase, and placing the rest of Leila's gifts out on the coffee table. Now all she had to do was wait. She was sure Leila would arrive at around 2 in the afternoon, and she checked her phone countless times, waiting to get a phone call to say that Leila was outside. The buzzer on Avery's apartment had been broken for so long that everyone living in the building had gotten used to their friends ringing before being let up.

At 2:30, there was still no word from Leila, and Avery was feeling anxious.

What if something happened to her? What if her phone was stolen or her car flipped, or she was in an accident? Avery thought, making herself feel sick just as she heard her phone ring.

"Hi," Avery quickly said, answering the phone almost immediately, sounding desperate but making Leila laugh.

"Hey, I'm out front," Leila replied casually, Avery racing to the door and buzzing her up. Avery hung up, knowing that the reception cut out when people used the elevator and opened her front door. She walked to the elevator door, decided against it, and quickly ran back to her apartment so that Leila wouldn't see her. Avery heard Leila's footsteps as she walked down the corridor towards the apartment and waited in the doorway.

"Welcome home," Avery said, laughing and opening her arms to Leila, walking toward her and wrapping her arms around her in a tight embrace. Leila smelled the sultry notes of Avery's perfume and relaxed into the embrace, her heart missing the woman more than she had let herself believe.

"Gosh, it feels good to be back," Leila sighed, resting her head on Avery's shoulder.

"Come on, let's get you inside. You must be exhausted after such a long drive," Avery said, taking Leila's bags and walking into the apartment, closing the door behind her, and putting them down.

"I got you a few homecoming gifts," Avery said, making Leila look at her curiously.

"You didn't need to, but I will never turn a gift down," Leila said, causing Avery to notice the change in how Leila received her presents.

The old Leila would have felt undeserving of

anything. I like this new version. She is more self-assured, Avery thought to herself as she led Leila to the living room and sat down on the couch.

"Wow, you have really outdone yourself, haven't you!" Leila exclaimed, making Avery laugh.

"I wasn't sure what to get you, so I got you, everything," Avery replied, accepting a donut Leila offered her.

"Yummy," Leila said, her little voice escaping and making Avery melt.

"I've missed you, baby girl. I'm so proud of you for going out into the world on your own for a while and figuring yourself out. But I'm really happy you came back to me," Avery admitted, Leila, moving closer to her to snuggle into her side.

"Same. It was weird at first, but I needed it to feel like the real me again. It didn't feel right not being around you, though," Leila replied, smiling at Avery and wondering how long it would take them to get back into their Mommy and little dynamic. Avery took another donut, Leila leaning forward and taking a bite.

"I know you only bought 12, so there'd be enough for you too," Leila giggled, making Avery feel playful.

"Maybe I did," Avery said, picking up another one and walking to the kitchen to grab a bottle of water. She thought for a moment before picking up Leila's sippy cup and holding it up, raising a questioning eyebrow. She didn't want to push Leila back into something she wasn't ready for, but she also wanted her baby girl back, relieved when Leila nodded yes.

"So, you want to just jump straight back in?" Leila giggled as Avery came back to sit down next to her.

"If that's something you want as well? I don't want to push you," Avery said. Leila smirked and pushed Avery backward.

"Like that?" Leila cheekily said as Avery sat back up, taken by surprise.

"I'm going to let you have that, but never again, little one," Avery said, pointing a finger to Leila, who yawned and checked her watch.

"It's only early afternoon, and I am exhausted," Leila said, resting her head on the back of the couch and closing her eyes.

"Well, if you feel like you want a little TLC, can Mommy give you a bath and get you ready for an early night?" Avery said, feeling that nervous knot tie back up in her stomach. She thought it was funny how Leila made her so self-conscious. Usually, she had the game of a stud, but something about this girl made her question herself more than any other girl ever had.

"I'd really like that," Leila replied, happily accepting the pacifier Avery put in her mouth before leading her to the bathroom.

"Gosh, Mommy is happy you are home with me, little one," Avery said as she began to undress Leila. She ran the bathwater and added bubbles, helping Leila into the tub before sitting on the floor next to her and watching as she played.

"Mommy's missed your little giggles," Avery said, resting her head on the side of the bath and happily smiling.

"Sorry, Mommy," Leila replied, reaching out to touch Avery's cheek. Avery kissed Leila's hand.

"Don't be, I'm just so happy you are happy and safe and feeling good," Avery replied. Reaching into the tub and beginning to wash Leila's back.

"You know something, Mommy," Leila said, taking her pacifier out of her mouth.

"No, what honey," Avery replied, gently taking the washcloth and washing Leila's face.

"I didn't wear a diaper the whole time, I only wanted you to diaper me, and if you couldn't then I didn't want to wear one," Leila said. Avery wasn't sure how to take the information, but she was happy that it clearly meant something to Leila.

"Well, good thing Mommy is here now, I can't have my little girl not diapered for bedtime!" Avery playfully exclaimed, taking Leila's hand and standing her up before rinsing her off.

"I still have all your stuff in my closet. I had hoped you'd come back to me," Avery said, drying Leila off and putting her hair in a ponytail.

"Cutie," Avery said, enjoying how gorgeous Leila looked before taking her hand and leading her to the bedroom. Leila sat on Avery's bed and crossed her legs, giggling when Avery pushed her backward.

"Lie down, baby girl," Avery lovingly instructed, making Leila smile as she enjoyed entering little space for the first time in over a month.

Chapter 9

"Such a beautiful girl," Avery said, putting on a pink singlet and kissing Leila's forehead.

"Are you a hungry baby girl, or did all those donuts Mommy get you make you full?" Avery said, laying next to Leila and letting her cuddle into her close. She had missed how physically needy Leila was, and she loved it.

"I'm full Mommy, I had a sandwich on my way home too," Leila said, closing her eyes.

"Alright. What jammies should Mommy wear tonight?" Avery said, knowing full well the ones that Leila was going to choose.

"The fluffy gray ones, Mommy," Leila cheerfully answered. These were the most snuggly pair of jammies Avery had, and whenever she wore them, Leila would cuddle up beside her.

"I thought so," Avery said, putting them on. Avery had half anticipated that she and Leila would have sex, so she had showered shortly before Leila had arrived. Coming into bed next to Leila, she wondered if Leila would want to suck on her nipple like she had seen in a video from her favorite website. The fear of rejection from Leila was strong, and Avery bit her lip, 95% sure that Leila would like it, but nervous all the same.

"Hey, baby," Avery hesitantly asked, causing Leila to look up at her with curious eyes.

"Yeah, Mommy?" Leila questioned, seeing that there was something that Avery clearly didn't feel confident discussing. Avery took out her phone and showed Leila a screenshot of the image of a couple, the little nursing in the arms of her Mommy. Leila didn't know what to say. She wasn't sure what Avery was trying to tell her.

"Do you like how it looks?" Avery asked, Leila, blushing and looking away.

"Yes," she softly said, feeling vulnerable and somewhat embarrassed.

"Do you want to try it with Mommy?" Avery asked, Leila's little side smile telling her all she needed to know.

"I don't have milk, but I still think it could be nice," Avery said, positioning Leila into place. Avery's breasts were a generous C-cup and were smaller than any girls' Leila had dated, including her own. She had nursed on Donna's breasts when they first got together, but it had slowly become less and less as the years went on.

Leila shook her head, wanting to get the image of Donna out of her mind and smile at herself, delighted that the feelings of rejection and hurt were able to be processed so quickly.

"Open that pretty mouth," Avery said, running her finger across Leila's lips and watching as she closed her mouth around Avery's nipple, sucking instinctively, causing Avery to moan involuntarily.

"Oh my, good girl," Avery moaned, catching her breath as she felt herself thrown into depths of Mommy space she hadn't experienced before. Her eyes glazed over, and when she refocused, she felt like a different version of herself, and she loved it.

Rocking Leila in her arms, Avery held her breast to Leila's lips, falling in love with how her mouth looked around her nipple and loved seeing how Leila's pupils dilated in pleasure.

"You like this too, hey baby girl?" Avery asked, Leila, nodding her head as she gently but hungrily sucked.

"I think that needs to become a part of the nightly routine," Avery said the following morning. Leila had fallen asleep with Avery's nipple in her mouth, Avery, with her arms wrapped around Leila's body. They had stayed like that until the morning when Leila had woken up first and had tiptoed to the living room. She sat on the couch and played on her phone. She didn't want to wake Avery up with the backlight of her game, but it hadn't taken Avery long to feel that Leila wasn't there.

"Same," Leila said, looking up from her game but quickly looking back down. Avery smiled, seeing Leila's thumbs working on overdrive to win the level she was on. Avery turned toward the coffee machine to see that Leila had already made her a latte and taking an apple from the fridge, Avery went to sit down next to Leila.

"After that level, put your phone away," Avery said, wanting her baby girl back.

"Ok, Mommy," Leila happily said, tapping so aggressively that Avery thought she might break her phone screen.

"Yes!" Leila exclaimed, putting her phone on the coffee table and turning to face Avery, who was looking at her in amusement.

"Why are you looking at me like that?" Leila asked, crossing her arms in playful defiance.

"Mommy can look at you any way I want," Avery replied, putting her latte down.

"I want to go over a few things with you like what you are going to do with your job, and I want a clearer understanding of what you want from me as your Mommy and girlfriend," Avery said, watching Leila's reaction.

"Alright," Leila said, looking down at herself and then looking back up at Avery.

"Yeah, fair point," Avery said, laughing and taking Leila's hand, leading her back into the bedroom.

"I love that if we were to have this discussion a few months ago, I simply wouldn't have been able to say what I want," Leila said as she undressed and put on a pair of off-cut denim shorts and a baggy long sleeve shirt. She put her hair in a cute messy ponytail and sat with Avery on the bed.

"Yeah, I know. I think it was so good of you to go out on your own and sort some stuff out. It was good for me too, I learned some stuff about myself and the different things I like," Avery said, bringing her knees up to her chest.

"Oh yeah? Like what, Mommy?" Leila sensually asked as she reached out and teased Avery's slit through her panties.

"Ha, like that little girls need to keep their hands to themselves," Avery replied, slapping

Leila's hand away, although getting wet.

"Ok, but like on a serious note. Tell me some stuff," Avery said, giving Leila a look of warning.

"Alright. I really loved sucking on your nipples last night, which was perfect for me. I think that I'm going to have a hard time wetting my diaper, but I want to try it and get comfortable with it if that's something you wouldn't hate. I don't really want stuffies, I want more like, mentally stimulating stuff like blocks and models I can build, but I still want my bunny to sleep with. I think that I like onesies more than a shirt and diaper cover, and the only other thing that I really want is for my hair to be stroked when we cuddle," Leila said, surprising herself by how open and honest she was being. Avery smiled at her as she wrote down a few things, not wanting to forget or leave out anything that Leila had said.

"I like that I can train you in something," Avery replied once she was finished writing.

"What about you?" Leila asked.

"I want to do things like pick you up from places, maybe work, or if you go out, I want to stay up and pick you up. Not in a creepy stalker way, but a, looking after you kind of way. If you'd like, I'd also want to end up moving in together, either here or we find a new place together. Apart from those things, I love everything we do, maybe have a routine for when I am working days and nights could be good as well, though," Avery replied.

"Sounds good to me. So," Leila said. It was a Saturday, and Avery had the day off.

"So?" Avery questioned, wondering what Leila was going to say.

"So, I know you have the day off. Wanna do something?" Leila asked, shyly smiling, hoping Avery wasn't sick and tired of her yet.

"I can't think of anything I would rather do more than hang out with you," Avery replied, making Leila clap her hands.

"So, maybe we could get dressed and go somewhere fun, like the beach or something?" Leila asked. Avery thought for a moment before answering.

"Could we make it a Mommy baby day? Or do you want to be a big girl?" Avery asked, making Leila giggle and blush.

"Mommy and baby day," she replied, delighting Avery.

"Well. Let's get you breakfast and then dressed. I know a few spots along the coastline that have some secluded spots, which will be perfect for you to play," Avery said, going to the kitchen.

"What are you hungry for?" Avery asked, fully prepared to cook up a storm.

"That apple looked really good, actually Mommy," Leila said, making Avery tilt her head to the side.

"Just because I want an apple doesn't mean that I am trying to change my body, Mommy. I'm actually happy with myself for the first time in years, and I want to have an apple just because I like how they taste. And they crunch and I like that too," Leila explained. Avery was happy. She never wanted Leila to be anything but herself.

"Alright. Do you want Mommy to cut it up for you?" Avery asked, watching as Leila nodded her head before she got up to go and get out of her adult clothes.

I've been in so many head spaces this morning. I am genuinely surprised I am keeping up! Leila thought to herself, giggling as she felt Avery's hands on her back.

"And what are you doing, little miss?" Avery said, placing the plate of apple slices down on the bedside table.

"I'm getting dressed," Leila said, giggling and running to the cupboard.

"We both know you are too little to dress yourself," Avery replied, taking a diaper down from the shelf, a pair of overalls and a pink shirt.

"Mommy, it's the day time!" Leila squealed, rolling around on the bed.

"Oh, I know that, but it's too hot to go to the beach right now. So now Mommy is going to diaper you, and you are going to wet it before we go anywhere. Don't worry. Mommy will get you all cleaned up before we go," Avery said, seeing the shock on Leila's face.

"Such a cute little thing," Avery said, grabbing Leila's ankles and pulling her down the bed and onto her back. Leila's surprised face made Avery smile.

"Didn't you think Mommy was so strong? You're my little girl, of course, Mommy can move you how I want to," Avery said, flexing her large biceps, making Leila giggle and blush.

"Ok, bottoms up," Avery said, tapping Leila on her thighs and waiting for her to lift up as Avery slid a diaper underneath her.

"First, some powder to make you all soft, we don't want to get rashies now do we," Avery said, Leila, shaking her head no. Avery rubbed the powder over Leila's body, making her giggle before she pulled the tabs firmly, fastening the diaper to Leila's waist. Leila closed her eyes and sighed in contented bliss. There was something so beautifully triggering in the way Avery touched her, and this simple act had thrown Leila into little space in only the way Avery knew how to do.

"Sit up for Mommy," Avery said, waiting for Leila to follow her instruction.

"Arms up," Avery said, pulling the t-shirt over Leila's head and pulling her arms through. Avery then helped Leila put her overalls on and made her giggle as she put her hair in a messy ponytail.

"My beautiful girl," Avery said. She bit her bottom lip for a moment before going back to the cupboard and taking out a pink bow hair tie, wrapping it around the one already in Leila's hair.

"Now you're finished," Avery said, ticking Leila all over and making her giggle.

"Mommy, don't I might," Leila said, stopping herself as she lay back and used her feet to try and keep Avery off her.

"You'll what sweet girl? Wet your diaper, that's kinda the point," Avery said, winking at her and making Leila blush.

"But right now?" Leila asked, the worried

look on her face making Avery's heart melt.

"No, it doesn't have to be right now, just sometime today when you feel ok about it. Then Mommy will get you all nice and clean, and we can go to the beach," Avery explained. Leila thought for a moment.

"But straight away? You'll make sure I'm clean straight away?" Leila nervously asked, Avery just nodding her head.

"I know you don't like to be a dirty baby girl. Mommy isn't going to let you be, don't worry," Avery said, wondering if keeping Leila in her wet diaper for five minutes could be used as a future punishment.

"Ok," Leila said, satisfied that she had an understanding of the situation and got off the bed.

"Can we go play now, please, Mommy?" Leila asked, her ponytail tilting to one side as she asked the question.

"Of course, baby girl. Mommy wants to see you crawl though," Avery instructed, watching as Leila obediently got onto her hands and knees and began to crawl.

"But what about bunny?" Leila suddenly said, stopping and almost getting run into by Avery.

"You mean, this bunny?" Avery said, holding out Leila's stuffie, making her giggle.

"Mommy knows everything," Leila happily said as she continued to crawl into the living room.

"Mommy knows a few things," Avery said, enjoying that Leila thought she was the most knowledgeable person in the world. When Leila reached the living room, she crawled over to the coffee table to took out the coloring in book and colors Avery had bought for her.

"Mommy is going to make a light snack, you need to finish eating your apple slices, and then you can have a bottle," Avery said, watching Leila from the kitchen.

"Mommy, do you think I need to look different," Leila said, taking Avery by surprise.

"No, what makes you say that," Avery said, stopping what she was doing and coming over to sit down next to Leila on the floor. She knew that Leila felt self-conscious about her weight, and it made her feel sad that she wasn't happy within herself 100% of the time.

"My 20year high school reunion is coming up in 6months, and it's all I can think about. I want to go, but I don't feel good about myself all the time yet. I get moments where I do, but I want those moments to be longer," Leila said, biting her bottom lip and blushing.

"What is it about yourself that you want to change? It's ok and healthy to evolve and adapt, but only if it is for the right reasons," Avery replied.

"I want to look more like this," Leila said, taking her phone out of her front pocket in her overalls and showing Avery a photo of a curvy model.

"I think that if I just lost a little extra weight, that would make me feel more like me. I also want to change my hair and get my eyelashes tinted. I kind of want to start taking care of my appearance a bit more. Like, the old me is in the past, and I want to make a new me. When we went out the first time, and I was all done up, I liked that, and I want to look like that a lot more," Leila said, shrugging her shoulders.

She's thought about this, Avery thought to herself as she looked at the woman in front of her, smiled, and reached out her hand to stroke her cheek.

"Alright, well, what do you want to start with?" Avery asked. She was constantly being surprised by Leila and liked that she was always on some sort of improvement journey.

"I think the easiest stuff to do first would be like getting my hair done and eyelashes tinted. I want to buy some new make-up and try some new looks. I think maybe I should get a personal trainer too. I just want to feel like my body can do what I want it to do," Leila replied, bringing her knees up to her chest.

"That makes sense," Avery replied, nodding in agreement.

"That was a very grown-up conversation for someone wearing a diaper," Avery quickly added, winking at Leila and getting up to go back into the kitchen.

Chapter 10

Leila took what felt like forever to eat the apple slices, Avery coming to sit on the couch and watch her color in, having to tell her every once in a while to eat a slice.

"I am Mommy!" Leila giggled as she picked up the last slice. Avery went on her phone and looked up award-winning hairstylists in the area. She had decided she could probably also enhance her appearance and try a new salon. Avery made two appointments online.

"Finally," Avery joked, making Leila giggle and bounce while she sat the way she always did when she was happy.

"Chocolate or vanilla baby?" Avery called from the kitchen, holding up two different protein powders. Leila tilted her head as she thought before pointing to the vanilla one before going back to her coloring in. Avery made up the shake, put it in a bottle, and can back to the couch, patting her lap and waiting for Leila to lay in her arms.

"Mommy's sweet girl," Avery cooed as Leila drank. Avery knew that before long, Leila would make her diaper wet, although she was almost sure Leila was trying to hold it.

"You know, good girls' who wet their diaper sometimes get treats," Avery said, making Leila's eyes sparkle from behind the bottle. Leila knew that Avery knew that she needed to go to the bathroom. Leila also knew that Avery knew she was trying to hold it.

"What sort of treats," Leila asked, pushing Avery's hand away, just for Avery to push the nipple of the bottle back into Leila's mouth.

"Shh, Mommy shouldn't hear girls who have a bottle in their mouths," Avery instructed. Leila stopped drinking, worried that if she continued, she would wet herself involuntarily. Avery smirked at her before raising an eyebrow and squeezing the bottle, causing the milky drink to fill her mouth.

"Don't be a bad girl little Leila or Mommy will have to spank you, and you will still have to make your diaper wet," Avery explained, Leila moaning in frustration, understanding that there was no way out of this. Leila finished her bottle, and Avery patted the front of her diaper, making her blush.

"Come on, Mommy knows you are desperate to go," Avery said, enjoying the embarrassment she was causing Leila but aware that Leila couldn't be pushed too much further.

"You play down on the floor with your toys while Mommy tidies the kitchen. And when I come back, you'd better have been a good girl," Avery instructed, making Leila nervous and shy. She watched as Leila got down on the floor and began playing with her bunny. Avery took her time, emptying the dishwasher and packing away the food into the fridge and cupboard before coming back down to Leila. She wanted to allow her to go in her own time.

Coming back down to the floor, Avery pulled Leila

into her lap and placed her hand on the front of her diaper, turning Leila around enough that she could see the frown on Avery's face.

"Mommy, I can't," Leila whined, in a vain attempt to sway Avery's mind on the matter.

"Hmm, I don't think that's the case," Avery plainly said as she pressed her hand against Leila's bladder, making her gasp.

"You can fight Mommy, or you can do what Mommy wants. But let me make myself very clear, if you fight Mommy, there will be consequences, and they'll really hurt," Avery whispered in Leila's ear, continuing to press into her.

"But Mommy," Leila said, biting her lip and beginning to cry.

"Don't try that baby girl. It won't work," Avery said, smirking as Leila stopped almost immediately, somewhat put out that Avery knew all her tricks.

"That's what I thought. Now come on, Mommy is here, and you can be a good girl for me," Avery said, redirecting Leila's mind to the command she had yet to obey. Leila shifted in Avery's arm, causing Avery to hold onto her firmly.

"You're about to be spanked, do you know that?" Avery said, grabbing Leila's breasts with both hands and squeezing them tightly. Leila pushed against Avery, trying to get away, only to be placed over Avery's thigh in one swift motion. Leila could feel herself almost give in as Avery's other thigh locked her in place, and her strong arm came crashing down on Leila's ass.

"Mommy!" Leila whined, trying to turn her head to look at Avery.

"Did Mommy say you could look at me? What was Mommy's instruction, Leila?" Avery sternly asked, bringing another blow onto Leila's ass.

"To wet my diaper," Leila said, feeling the sting of Avery's spanking.

"And did you listen to Mommy?" Avery asked, making Leila mad that she already knew the answer.

"No," Leila whined, copping another spank.

"No, what?" Avery growled.

"No, Mommy," Leila answered, Avery, stopping for a moment to rub between Leila's thighs.

"Are you going to be a good girl now?" Avery asked, squeezing her thighs tightly around Leila and keeping her hand in place as she waited for Leila's response.

"But Mommy," Leila said, Avery, letting go and getting up, taking Leila by the wrist and leading her into the bedroom.

"You asked me what this was for last night," Avery said, referring to the bolt in the wall with the O ring attached to it. Leila looked at her waiting for what was inevitably coming next.

"It's for when you're naughty and need time to think about your actions," Avery said, taking a rope and tying Leila's wrists together before threading the rope through the ring and pulling down, forcing Leila's arms to stretch above her head. With Leila's body elongated, Avery kicked her ankles apart, tying her thighs in a way that forced them apart.

"Mommy," Leila moaned, feeling her clit harden.

"Now, you want to be my sweet, obedient girl?" Avery mocked, kissing Leila on the cheek as she lubed a vibrator and unclipped the straps on Leila's overalls.

"We could be at the beach right now, but you wanted to test Mommy. Silly girl that is never a good idea," Avery said, pulling the overalls down until Leila's diaper was exposed. Pulling the front out, Avery slipped the thick vibrating dildo between Leila's puffy pussy lips, angling the tip, so it was on her clit, also simulating her to wet herself.

"You can stay like that until I get what I want. But just know, that for every five minutes that I don't get my way, I'm adding another toy to you," Avery said, pulling on Leila's nipples before walking out the door and closing it behind her, leaving Leila in the darkened room alone. Avery sighed as she walked back to the living room and began tidying away Leila's toys. She liked that Leila was so stubborn, it made training her all the more fun. Leila, on the other hand, was having a hard time and was surprised that she didn't want to give into Avery's commands as obediently as she had done in the past.

"So, let's see," Avery said, feeling Leila's diaper, shrugging her shoulders when she felt that it was dry.

"You really want to see what Mommy can do, don't you, baby?" Avery asked, pushing a paci gag in Leila's mouth when she tried to reply.

"No, I didn't really want to hear your answer," Avery said, fastening the gag in place before taking out a butt plug and lubing it up slowly.

"Yeah, you know where this is going, don't you," Avery said, watching as Leila tried to pull her thighs together, making Avery laugh.

"Nice try sweetheart," Avery whispered, pulling the back of Leila's diaper out and slipping her hand against Leila's ass. Avery grabbed her ass cheeks and forced them open before she pushed the butt plug into Leila, making Leila gasp and moan as Avery pushed it in place.

"I thought that maybe I would be finished by now, but I can see you still have that look of defiance in your eye," Avery said, taking the nipple clamps and dangling them in front of Leila's face.

"Oh, what's this?" Avery said, seeing that Leila wet her diaper. Leila pushed herself out toward Avery, willing to follow her command so that she wouldn't have to suffer the pain of the clamps, making Avery laugh.

"I'll start with these next time, I think," Avery said, discovering what Leila hated most of all. She cupped Leila's face in her hands, rubbed her cheeks with her thumbs, and kissed her nose.

"See, it wasn't so bad was it," Avery said, forcing herself to stay true to her promise that she would clean Leila up straight away.

"I have half a mind to keep you here as a lesson not to make me have to wait so long for you to obey me. But Mommy isn't a liar, so I'll clean you up right now. But if you make me wait this long again, I'll make you wait for the same time you made me. Fair?" Avery said, delighting in the shock and fear in Leila's eyes and the nodding of her head as a shiver ran through her body.

"Good," Avery replied, untying Leila but keeping the gag in, laughing when Leila pawed at it.

"Oh no, you can keep that in. I like you quiet," Avery said, Leila, looking away sheepishly, knowing that she didn't want to undergo another punishment. Avery took off the diaper, vibrator, and butt plug and took Leila's hand, leading her into the bathroom.

"Arms up," Avery said as she lifted Leila's shirt off, unclipping her bra and throwing it on the floor before lightly patting her ass, directing her into the shower.

"Mommy is going to join you," Avery said, stripping down quickly and turning the water on, letting Leila stand in the corner until she found the right temperature.

"We are going to wash our hair as well, and if you are a good girl, when we are done here, you can take that out," Avery said, pulling Leila's hair out and beginning to wash her body. Avery slid her hands over Leila's curves, kissing down her body and making her nipples hard.

"And here I thought you were a sweet innocent little girl," Avery whispered as she let her hand slip between Leila's thighs, smirking as Leila spread her legs and let Avery stroke her clit. Avery loved that Leila couldn't reply, watching as her body told her all she needed to hear.

"Yes, that's right, sway those hips for Mommy," Avery coaxed, watching as Leila tried to gain a stronger touch from Avery. Pushing her against the wall, Avery stroked further along Leila's lips and pushed passed the folds of her pussy, feeling her wetness at her entrance.

"If you scream, Mommy will slap your face. Do you understand me?" Avery sternly said, watching as Leila nodded her head, her eyes suddenly going wide as Avery quickly pushed into her cunt, filling her pussy with two fingers and beginning to curl them inside of her.

"Uh uh, Mommy said no," Avery reminded Leila as she stifled her squeal, turning it into a low groan of pleasure.

"You are so lucky to have a Mommy who knows how to treat her princess," Avery whispered in Leila's ear as she held her tight and fingered her pussy, making quick work of bringing on an orgasm. Leila bent her head forward, her body shaking and her thighs almost giving way as Avery made her cum within minutes. Slowly her rhythm, Avery took a step back, ungagged Leila, and smiled as she saw her girlfriend catch her breath.

"You're going to need a lie down after the mind games I just put you through," Avery said, smirking as she looked at Leila's mentally exhausted face.

"Come on, baby girl," Avery said, taking Leila's hand and drying her off before letting her crawl into bed naked.

"I just want Mommy," Leila whined, reaching out for Avery, who was busy getting dressed in her bikini, putting house clothes on over the top before coming to rest next to Leila.

"Mommy's here," Avery said as Leila buried her face into Avery's neck and breathed in deeply. Avery wrapped her arms around Leila, enjoying how lucky she felt to have her all to herself and closed her eyes.

I'll just lay here for a moment, Avery thought, feeling herself begin to fall asleep but unable to wake herself back up.

Chapter 11

"Wake up sleeping beauty," Avery said an hour later. Leila had fallen asleep in her arms and was sucking her thumb in her sleep.

"Mommy," Leila sleepily said as she slowly woke up.

"We need to wake up, or we won't make it to the beach, and we won't be able to get to sleep tonight," Avery explained, causing Leila's eyes to go wide.

"The beach!" Leila exclaimed, making Avery laugh.

"Yes, come on. I'm ready," Avery said, gently rolling Leila out of her arms and getting up.

"I can't go in the water, I don't have a swimsuit here," Leila said, putting on a pair of shorts and a flowy top. Avery raised her eyebrows and took out a bag from under her bed.

"Maybe you didn't think you had a

swimsuit, but I have one," Avery said, passing Leila that bag, her confused face making Avery laugh.

"You got me, swimmers?" Leila asked, Avery, nodding her head.

"So, you had this beach trip planned all along!" Leila squealed, taking out the swimmers and being pleasantly surprised at the choice Avery had made.

"These are cute," Leila said as she looked at the colorful striped one piece with the plunging neckline.

"Try them on, and if you hate them, then we can return them," Avery said as Leila undressed and put the swimmers on.

"They are actually really great, Mommy," Leila replied, looking herself over in the mirror. She wasn't sure how Avery did it, but she knew the perfect way to dress her so that her best features were highlighted, and the parts of herself she wanted to change where hidden.

"I love them," Leila softly said, turning around and looking at Avery.

"Are you alright?" Avery said, tilting her head to look at Leila.

"Yeah, you are just really amazing," Leila quietly confessed, causing Avery's arms to be wrapped around her in a big bear hug.

"You are really amazing," Avery said, kissing Leila on the tip of her nose and winking at her.

"Come on, get dress, I'll wait for you in the car," Avery said playfully as she half skipped out the door.

Avery and Leila held hands as they walked down the secluded path to the beach, enjoying the feeling of the sand between their toes. There was still two hours before sunset, and the water was warm after a day of the hot sun burning down on it.

"Are you going to come in?" Avery asked Leila as she stripped her clothes off. Leila took the time to admire her girlfriend's body. Avery's athletic form, highlighted by the afternoon sun, reminded Leila of the fitness models she had begun following on social media.

"Yeah, in a minute," Leila said, checking to see if anyone else was nearby. Avery caught on to what Leila was doing and came to sit in front of her.

"You are gorgeous, and you are valid, and you are mine, so I will protect you, all of you, your grown-up self, and you're little self, all of you. Ok?" Avery said, looking Leila in the eye and making her bashfully smile and nod her head.

"Ok," Leila said, giving in to Avery's words. She got up and undressed, nervously looked out along the shoreline, and smiled as she saw Avery's hand extended out to her.

Just take the leap, Leila said to herself, taking Avery's hand and walking down to the water.

Leila couldn't remember the last time she had been at the beach, let alone in the water, and as she tasted the saltiness of the ocean, a new sense of freedom washed over her body. Dipping her head under the water, Leila felt as the waves tumbled over her body, coming up for air and flipping her hair back. Running her hands through her wet hair, she caught Avery looking lustfully at her.

"Like what you see, Mommy?" Leila teased, watching as Avery swam up close to her.

"Yeah, I really do," Avery said, feeling Leila's body under the water, making her laugh.

"What were you doing for all that time you were away?" Avery suddenly asked, taking Leila by surprise.

"I just kind of isolated myself for a few weeks and let my mind stop trying to distract myself from all the shit I was trying to distract it with," Leila honestly replied.

"What did you do?" Leila asked. Leila ducked under the water as a wave came crashing into them, making Avery laugh as she got tumbled around in the water. Coming up for air, Avery wiped the water from her eyes and looked back toward the shoreline.

"I drank mostly. Was a bit of a jerk to a new woman at work and just generally felt miserable and sorry myself," Avery replied, making Leila frown.

"I'm so sorry," she said, causing Avery to shake her head.

"Don't be. Mommy's crappy coping skills is her problem. I'm happy you got what you needed out of it. I'm even happier you wanted to come back to me afterward," Avery explained, making Leila laugh as she began to head back toward the sand.

"What is it?" Avery said when Leila suddenly stopped swimming.

"I just want to stay here a little longer," Leila replied. She knew she wasn't meant to lie, so she decided just to withhold a part of the whole truth. But Avery knew her better than that.

"And why don't you want to go back in yet?" Avery asked, not satisfied with getting a half-truth. Leila looked to where another couple was putting their things down and bit her bottom lip.

"I know that woman," Leila said, the fear in her voice making Avery frown.

"An ex?" Avery asked, her Mommy space flooding her being. She felt the protectiveness flowing through her veins. She loved this feeling as it always made her feel as though she had superhuman strength.

"The ex," Leila said, emphasizing the word the. From what Leila had told Avery, Avery knew her ex Donna was a real piece of work.

"Ok. Hold Mommy's hand, and do not speak to her, alright. Do not look at her. Look at Mommy because when we get out of this water, I am going to be talking to you, and you know how much I hate it when you don't look at me when I am speaking," Avery instructed. Leila was happy that she was taking the lead with this and not making Leila do it alone.

"Thanks, Mommy," Leila said, grateful that Avery was so protective.

"What you want to do when we get home," Avery said the moment they stepped onto the shore. Donna was to the left of Leila, meaning when she was looking at Avery, she couldn't see Donna at all. Avery, on the other hand, could see both Leila and Donna and was glad because when Donna began to walk towards Leila, Avery could switch spots with her.

"Look at the ground, baby girl," Avery said. Usually, she didn't care to have her baby following such orders as she felt it was more for subs than littles, but in this case, she was going to make an exception.

"You have no business here, fuck off," Avery said before Donna could open her mouth to speak, leaving her speechless and putting a huge smirk on Leila's face.

"Get your things and let's go," Avery calmly said, holding Leila's hand and walking to the car, leaving Donna to stand dumbfounded behind them.

"Mommy," Leila giggled, still looking at the ground. Avery happily smirked that she could protect her little girl.

"You can look up now, honey," Avery said when they were in the car and driving home.

"Oh my god, that was so good!" Leila squealed, clapping her hands and making Avery laugh.

"Sometimes the best thing to do is leave it up to Mommy," Avery said, holding onto Leila's hand and turning on the radio as they drove home.

Chapter 12

They drove home in silence, just listening to the radio. Leila looked out the window, thinking of how far she had come, happy to be under Avery's care.

"We're home, sweetheart," Avery said, unsure if Leila was asleep or not.

"I know, Mommy," Leila softly replied, turning to face Avery as she took her seatbelt off.

"My sleepy girl," Avery said, reaching out and stroking Leila's cheek affectionately. She knew the emotional toll of seeing Donna would weigh heavily on Leila, even if it were a successful encounter. Avery also knew that Leila would be in a fragile state of mind, and she wondered if that would make it easier or harder for her to get into little space, potentially wetting her diaper once more.

"I'm not very hungry, Mommy," Leila said,

walking into the apartment. Avery opened the door, and Leila dropped her bag before going to the couch and sitting down.

"No, you don't, come on," Avery said, holding her hand out to Leila. Leila rolled her eyes at Avery before submitting to her wishes and standing back up, taking her hand and going to the bathroom.

"I know you might not be hungry, but you still need to have a shower and get all the sea salt off that little body," Avery said, stripping Leila naked and running the shower. Avery liked that Leila wasn't trying to fight her and was sleepy, allowing Avery to take charge.

"You can get into some nice jammies, have a bottle and cuddle with Mommy in bed, baby girl," Avery said, making Leila close her eyes and smile as Avery washed her body. Not wasting any time, Avery quickly washed Leila, running the warm water over her body to rinse her clean and turned the water off.

"Go and stand over there and wait for

Mommy," Avery said, pointing to the towel she had put down on the floor before disappearing into the bedroom. Leila knew what was coming, a diaper and onesie, and she waited with her towel wrapped around her for Avery to return.

"Here, lay down," Avery said, opening up another towel and placing it over the floor so that Leila wouldn't get cold. Leila obeyed, laying on the fluffy pink towel and felt Avery begin to diaper her.

"I know it was a warm day, but the news said it was going to get cold tonight, so you need to keep your sockies on," Avery said, pulling the onesie over Leila's head and putting on her socks.

"Ok, Mommy," Leila sleepily replied. Avery smirked.

She must be really tired if she isn't going to fight me on the socks, she thought to herself, knowing how much Leila hated wearing socks to bed. Avery led Leila to the bedroom, feeling Leila slowly dragged her feet behind her.

"Come on, sleepyhead," Avery said, turning

back to see Leila sucking her thumb. She pushed Leila into bed, watching her snuggle into the bed sheets immediately and close her eyes.

"Mommy will be back shortly," Avery said, guessing that Leila would be asleep before she came back.

Avery walked into the kitchen and prepared a bottle for Leila. She warmed the milk and put a scoop of vanilla protein powder in the shaker before shaking it up, then pouring it into a baby bottle. Avery knew that she would be awake for a long time yet, so she didn't bother making herself anything to eat. Walking back into the room, she watched as Leila stirred, and Avery climbed into bed with her and pulled her into her arms, cradling her.

"It's just Mommy," Avery whispered, pushing the bottle into Leila's mouth, feeling her resist. Leila scrunched up her face, before rolling into Avery and began to drink.

"Good girl," Avery said, gently rocking Leila as she drank. Avery thought about what Leila had said about wanting to become the best version of herself and wondered how she could help.

I don't think I should train her. She might feel embarrassed she can't do something and try to push herself and hurt herself. Maybe I should get her a personal trainer, someone really lovely and kind, that doesn't show off their body so much. I don't think she'd like that, Avery thought.

But then again, maybe group fitness would be good. That way she can meet some new people, maybe make some friends and then have people to bounce ideas about different exercises and nutrition off? Avery questioned, slightly overwhelmed by the choices. The last thing she wanted was to suggest something and have Leila think that Avery didn't like her body or that she was in some way flawed or ugly. Leila stirred, causing Avery to be shaken from her thoughts and look down to see Leila's big eyes staring back at her.

"Baby girl?" Avery questioned, seeing the startled look in Leila's eyes.

"Mommy, I," Leila began to say, before

biting her bottom lip and looking down toward her diaper.

"Oh sweetie, that's ok, Mommy will clean you up," Avery reassuring said. She placed the bottle down and rolled back the bedsheets.

"I don't like it, Mommy," Leila whined, making Avery smile.

"I know, that's why Mommy is changing you straight away," Avery replied, putting Leila's pacifier in her mouth and began to change her diaper. Leila shut her eyes tight, hating the feeling of being so exposed and patiently waited until Avery had a clean, dry diaper fastened to her body.

"There, all done, sweet girl," Avery said, letting Leila snuggle into her once more.

"Night night angel," Avery said, feeling Leila grab at her breast. Avery took her shirt and bra off, holding her breast to Leila's mouth and sighing when she felt Leila begin to suck on her nipple as she fell back asleep.

Chapter 13

"How serious are you about wanting to get into fitness baby, because I saw a great deal online if you're still interested," Avery called from the kitchen bench a week later. Leila had stayed at Avery's apartment since she had returned, and the two had slowly developed a comfortable dynamic, and smooth routine.

"Pretty serious," Leila replied, looking up from her laptop. She had begun to write for a very influential blog and was typing furiously to meet a deadline.

"What's the deal?" She added, putting her laptop top lid down slightly and giving Avery her full attention.

"10 group sessions for $100. They train just down the road at the park on the corner," Avery said, grabbing Leila's curiosity.

"That's cheap," Leila said, thinking about

how it would feel to be able to move more freely and feel more confident in herself.

"When does the offer begin?" Leila asked, standing up from the chair, stretching and coming over to Avery, who sipped her second espresso.

"Next week," Avery said, making Leila smile.

"Well, we better go shopping then. I'll need some activewear," Leila smirked, happy to feel in control of her life. Avery playfully slapped her ass, and Leila turned around with the gleam in her eye that Avery had hoped to elicit.

"We can't," Avery said, enjoying the smirk Leila gave when she was told she couldn't have something. Leila always took that as a challenge to work for something harder.

"You'll miss your deadline," Avery continued, pushing her chair in and grabbing Leila by her neck, pulling her in close.

"You better be fast then," Leila replied, feeling Avery's hands on her hips and turning her around, bending her over the kitchen table and pulling her sweat pants off.

"Yes," Avery hissed, grabbing at Leila's ample ass and thighs, relishing how soft and smooth they were. Leila tried to turn around, but Avery placed her strong arm down on Leila's back, holding her in place as she reached around and began to tease Leila's clit through her panties.

"Someone's wet," Avery whispered, making Leila shiver as she was touched. Avery continued to slowly stroke Leila, feeling how her clit slowly grew into a swollen nub before she pushed her fingers into Leila's mouth, making her suck them.

"Get them wet, baby girl. Mommy wants them wet," Avery slowly said, keeping Leila in place by pushing her down with her hips. Leila obeyed, moaning as she felt herself being taken by Avery.

"Spread your legs for me," Avery instructed, causing a tremor of pleasure to run through Leila's body. Obediently, Leila spread her thighs, feelings Avery pull her panties to the side and placed her wet fingers over Leila's clit, rubbing softly. Avery breathed heavily, reaching into her pants and pulling out the strap on cock she was packing. Pushing it between Leila's pussy lips, parting them roughly, Avery pulled back and spat on it before sliding it back, feeling Leila press back on her. Avery grabbed Leila's hair, pushed the tip of the strap on into her, and waited for Leila's pussy to fully open up to her.

"Mommy loves how tight you are little one," Avery moaned as she gently pulled Leila back down on top of her. Avery was now laying on the floor with Leila sitting on top of her, taking the long fake cock up her cunt.

"That's it. Grind that pussy on Mommy," Avery said, feeling Leila begin to twerk on her lap. Avery could feel her own juices begin to flow as Leila worked herself toward an orgasm, moaning and bouncing on Avery. Avery reached for a vibrating butt plug and lubed it while Leila tried desperately to make herself cum. In one quick motion, Avery stuffed the butt plug into Leila's ass, feeling her clit tingle as she heard Leila groan as the unexpected intruder began to vibrate inside of her. Leila grabbed Avery's shins as she came, Avery slapping her ass hard with both hands.

"Did I say you could stop?" Avery growled, curious to see how much Leila could take.

"No, sorry, Mommy," Leila replied, beginning to twerk once again. Avery turned the butt plug up, causing Leila's pussy to drip over Avery's lap, just the way she liked.

"No, that's right, I didn't," Avery replied, slapping Leila's ass once more.

"Faster," Avery added, looking around Leila's back and enjoying watching her tits bounce as she worked herself toward another orgasm. Avery couldn't decide if she wanted Leila to have the satisfaction or not as she watched her. The way her back arched, pushed her full breasts out, her hair swept to one side and her lip red from the way she bit it made Avery mesmerized.

I don't even know who is using who at this point, Avery thought to herself in amusement as she watched Leila come hard for the second time.

"Stop," Avery suddenly commanded, impressed that Leila frozen mild twerk. Avery watched how Leila's juices dripped down the shaft and onto the harness. Slowly pushing up, Avery filled Leila once again, sitting up and wrapping her arms around the woman.

"Mommy's little slut," Avery whispered in Leila's ear, holding her tight as she bent her legs and stood up, impressed with herself for being able to hold onto Leila as she did so. Avery gently put Leila's feet back down on the floor, pulled out of her in one quick motion, and smirked as Leila's juices squirted onto the floor.

"You know, a mean Mommy might make you lick that up," Avery said, remembering a video she watched a few days ago, deciding that she wasn't going to make Leila do that by the look in her eye.

"But I'm not that mean," Avery said, undoing the harness and winking at Leila before they headed to the shower.

"So, what sort of thing were you thinking?" Avery said two hours later, as they walked through the doors of a big sports department store. Leila had thought this would be fun, like the shopping they did when they found dresses, but as she looked around, she felt out of her depth.

"I guess I was just looking for something like this," she quietly said, looking around wide-eyed and showing Avery the photos she had screen-shotted. Avery looked through the photos and smiled.

"This is some cool stuff, baby," she encouragingly said. Leila gave her a small smile and was glad when Avery took her hand and began to take the lead.

"I don't really know what I am meant to be looking for or like, where even to start," Leila timidly said, melting Avery's heart.

"I know, honey, that's why I am here," Avery replied, stroking Leila's cheeks with her thumbs, making her face go red.

"Avery," Leila half hissed, worried that

someone might see them. Avery just giggled and began to flick through the clothing racks and found items that were as close to the ones which Leila had shown her.

"What about this?" Avery suggested seeing a shirt she thought Leila might like. Leila just nodded her head, feeling more confident now that she could see her outfits coming together.

"So, we have three pairs of tights, five shirts, some socks, and now we need some sports bras and shoes," Avery said, ticking things off the list she had created.

"Thanks for this," Leila said, taking Avery's hand and looking at her with the vulnerable eyes, which always melted Avery's heart.

"Baby girl, I wouldn't be anywhere else. You need me, I'm there," Avery replied, kissing the top of Leila's head.

"And maybe, a few caps," Leila said, picking up a cap and putting it on, causing Avery to raise an eyebrow.

"Mommy likes," Avery said, making Leila

blush as they head to the sports bra section.

"I don't think any of these will fit me," Leila said, a worried look on her face.

"It's not about the size, baby. It's about the fit. You have to find the fit that suits you best you worry about the size after that," Avery explained, making Leila smile. They tried on several bras, finally finding the fit which Leila felt the most comfortable in and put three of them into their shopping cart.

"I had no idea that it could be so, fun," Leila said, surprised at how enjoyable the experience had turned out to be. The staff were friendly and helpful, no one looked at her like she didn't belong and what was best of all, there were so many options for her to choose from.

"So, shoes?" Leila questioned, looking around to find Avery already holding up a pair of shoes.

"These are cool," Avery said, showing Leila the blue and yellow pair, making Leila laugh.

"I was thinking of something a little more

subtle," Leila laughed, picking up a pair of gray and pink Nike Metcon 5's. Avery raised her eyebrows, impressed with Leila's choice before getting the sales assistant's attention.

"Nice. I want a pair," Avery said, seeing them on Leila, who laughed.

"These are so cool," Leila said in her little voice the moment the assistant was gone. Avery agreed and put them into the shopping cart, before heading toward the register.

"It's a good thing that the class is so cheap because the sports gear cost a small fortune," Leila said as they drove home.

"Yeah, but now that you have everything you need unless you do a big shop like that again, you'll only pick up a few things at a time from now on," Avery replied as she watched Leila look at her new shoes. Avery smiled. She loved that she could help Leila become the person she wanted to become.

"So. When is the reunion?" Avery asked, wanting to know how much time they still had.

"Like six months away. I think that gives me enough time to get myself sorted. I don't want to change too much. I like how I look for the most part. I just want to feel more energetic and be a bit healthier. I don't want abs or muscular thighs, no offense," Leila laughed, realizing that she was describing Avery.

"Oh yeah, none taken," Avery laughed.

"No, it's fine. I know you want to look like the curvy models online. I'm just happy that you like my body," Avery said, realizing for the first time that she was slightly body conscious when it came to Leila's approval.

Everyone is insecure sometimes, Avery thought to herself, reminding herself of the self-help phrase she had read earlier in the day.

"Yeah, I think that is more who I am," Leila said, Avery, smiling at they pulled into the driveway.

"Ok. I have more work to do than I first thought," Leila panted, walking into the apartment.

Avery was sitting on the couch watching a movie on her laptop and smiled as she saw Leila stumble into the kitchen and take out a bottle of water.

"So, good?" Avery asked, pausing the movie and closing the lid.

"So good, but oh my goodness. So like, these girls can do so much stuff. They are machines!" Leila said, enjoying the afterglow of the session as the endorphins flooded her body.

"And I just feel all. I don't even know, happy?" Leila asked, making Avery laugh.

"Those are called endorphins, and you get that hormone released when you work out. This is good, baby! I'm so happy you liked it," Avery explained, getting up and sitting next to Leila on the bench stools.

"Yeah. It was really cool. Everyone is super nice, and I learned a lot already," Leila said before kicking her shoes off and sighing.

"Now I feel tired," she said, looking thoughtful as she felt the strange now emotions for the first time.

"Do you need Mommy to look after you?" Avery asked, hoping that she would say yes. Leila just nodded her head but giggled as Avery jumped up and grabbed her hand.

"Shower and naps," Avery said, Leila happily following behind.

"Ok, Mommy," Leila replied, yawning and closing her eyes as she walked.

***

"You look beautiful," Avery said six months later on the night of Leila's reunion. Leila had been to the hair salon and had also had her makeup professionally done. She had taken one of the dresses Avery had bought for her on their first date to the seamstress to be taken in. As the red sequined dress glittered under the lights, Leila buckled her heels and looked up at Avery.

"Well, a little bit of thanks goes to you," Leila said, winking at Avery, who beamed.

"I am really proud of you," Avery said,

tearing up and making Leila laugh.

"Why?" Leila asked, standing up, her heels making her taller than Avery for the first time.

"Because. You did it. You were in such a shitty place when we first met, and you did what you needed to do to become the person you needed to become. I would have loved you forever, but it was never about me, it was about you, and you looked at your life and who you wanted to become, and you made changes until you got there. Now you have a successful online presence, people follow your fitness tips, and you are an advocate for what a strong, healthy, and empowered woman can look like. Plus, you've got these great tits," Avery said, making the conversation slightly light by grabbing Leila's breasts and motorboating them, making Leila laugh.

"But on a serious note, I am really proud of you. You make me want to be a better person, somebody who is more aligned with who I truly am, and not somebody who just reacts to the world around them," Avery said, pulling a long rectangle box from her back pocket.

"So, in light of all your success, I wanted to give you something which hopefully shows you how inspired and grateful I am to have you in my life," Avery said, placing the box in Leila's hands.

"It's a good thing this makeup is waterproof," Leila said, before opening the box and gasping. Her eyes were dazzled by the diamond bracelet, clearly over 2carats, and set in white gold.

"Mommy," Leila said softly, looking at the beautiful bracelet.

"Do you like it?" Avery said, watching Leila's face.

"Yes. Of course I love it!" Leila exclaimed, smiling widely at Avery, who took it out of the box and fastened it to Leila's wrist.

"Turn it on its side," Avery said, wanting to show Leila the engraving.

"Mommy's always here," Leila read out loud, having to fan her eyes as they began to water.

"I love you," Leila said, kissing Avery on the mouth and feeling her heart pound deeply.

"I love you too, darling," Avery said, delighted with her life, the beautiful woman standing before her.

Who is Tina Moore?

Tina Moore has enjoyed the lifestyle of a Mommy Domme for several years. She began secretly exploring kink and BDSM in her youth and found her love of being a strict Mommy Domme in early 2000. Tina Moore slowly became more comfortable and confident through making friends in the community and exploring the lifestyle and now openly celebrates being a Mommy Domme to her little.

Before becoming an author, Tina Moore worked in the finance sector, but it was through the encouragement of her current little that she took the leap and wrote her first MDLG book, Nancy's Little One.

From then on, Tina Moore continued to combine her experiences and desires, as well as the sweet and naughty things her baby girl does, to bring you tantalizing and salacious stories about both MDLG and DDLG relationships and the ABDL littles and middles who enjoy them.

Follow her on:

Author Page on Amazon

Instagram @tinamoore.kdp